The Guardian

Book 3 of The Mender Trilogy

Jennifer Marchman

Stående Bjørn Press

The Guardian, Book 3 of the Mender Trilogy

Edition 1.0

Cover art by Oliver Bennett of More Visual Ltd.

Print ISBN: 9798850921538

Stående Bjørn Press
Austin, Texas, USA

For the people who died at the Battle of Coleto Creek and Goliad, both sides.

Contents

Content Warning

This novel is intended for an adult audience, deals with mature themes, confronts age-old conflicts, contains some language, and occasionally depicts violence, including brief scenes of sexual violence.

Any misplaced commas are unintentional but probably deserve a warning as well.

Prologue

Dear Reader,

What you have in your hands is *The Guardian*, a novel comprising the third installment of *The Mender Trilogy*. If you've not read *The Mender* (or *The Captive*) yet, you might want to start there.

But, if you're bound and determined to proceed to the end of the story — 'cause dang it, the end is always the most exciting (or maybe you need a refresher) — let me bring you up to speed:

Mender Eva, a true believer in the cult of Lux Libera, has dedicated her life to merging the multiverse's reality into the one True timeline. Partnered with fellow Mender Tophe, she travels through time and space to complete missions for her organization, often thwarting the good deeds of history's heroes. Highly skilled in martial arts, culture, and languages, Eva and Tophe boast an unblemished record of success and hope to be promoted to new leadership positions.

Tasked with a new mission, Eva and Tophe are accidentally separated during their journey. Eva sustains a head injury and finds herself stranded in the right place, but at the wrong time: 1835 Tejas y Coahuila. Jim, a discontented former Comanche captive, discovers Eva on his property and nurses her back to health. As Eva recovers, she worries she has permanently lost her ability to travel. She pitches in on Jim's farm, earning her keep while pretending to have damaged memories of who she is.

Despite believing Jim is only a Fated shadow of the True line and having taken a vow of celibacy, her growing friendship with Jim deepens into an undeniable attachment. Eva's love for Jim forces her to question everything she has been taught to believe about the nature of reality. Eventually, she confesses who and what she really is. Though she will face execution for apostasy if discovered, Eva renounces her faith to marry Jim.

Since his unexpected return to Anglo society, Jim has made a good-faith effort to establish himself in the community as a farmer, but his heart remains with his adoptive family's nomadic way of life. When the wealthiest plantation in Austin's Colony is raided and the owners murdered, Jim and Eva flee to Jim's Comanche village, avoiding a vengeful mob. Eva is welcomed by Jim's brothers and their wives but struggles to come to terms with the atrocities she has committed in her past and to adjust to a new life, new customs, and new moral code. Though used to living in a strict society, Eva chafes under Jim's high-handed shift in demeanor toward her as he conforms with what he believes to be the ideal Comanche warrior. As the weeks pass, she grows uneasy about her choices and her powerlessness to prevent the futures she knows are possible in this timeline.

Unable to forget about Tophe, she decides she must stop him from completing their mission. She travels into the midst of the Texas Revolution to save Francisca Alavez, known to the future as the Angel of Goliad, and hopes to expose the lies of Lux Libera to her former partner in the process.

Book 3 opens with Eva and Pump traveling to El Copano, and Jim is taking Pump's wife, Jane, to relatives in Louisiana.

Enjoy!

—Jennifer

Chapter 1

Jim

"It's nice to have you here again," Jane said over the rattle of the wagon.

Jim glanced at her with a smile. She'd been like a mother after Pump had found him. A smothering, opinionated, overbearing one, but he didn't doubt her love for him. He imagined she must see his parents when she looked at his face. He hadn't realized how much he had missed her or how pleased it would make him that she accepted Eva without question.

Pump had entrusted him to take Jane to Louisiana, safely away from the coming revolution, though Jim's heart traveled with Eva and the older man to El Copano to protect the Angel of Goliad. Every new mile that separated them added to his misgivings about letting Eva journey to a battlefield without him, regardless of the cause or the logic of her plans. He cared nothing for Tophe or the fate of people he'd never meet.

Fortunately, his companion did most of the talking. Jane told him of Pump's travels, her sons and their children, and the new babies that had been born in the community. "All hale and hearty, mothers, too," she said with justified pride.

"How are you faring all alone on the farm these days?"

"Well, I'll tell you, I'm finding it harder to keep up with everything. I'm trying to convince Pump to move us into San Felipe, but he likes our privacy."

Jim wondered how she took the loneliness. After growing up in a village, his breath caught at the thought of ever having to return to a solitary farming life.

By mid-morning, they reached San Felipe de Austin, and Jim widened his eyes at the sight. Men and women walked with long-strided purpose, heads down against the icy wind, and snaking lines formed down the boardwalks at the general stores. Anvils rang a frenzied tattoo from the blacksmiths, and horses waited to be shod. Rifles stood ready at hand. Even the Tejanos' Spanish Town on the eastern edge of the city buzzed with rumor.

Jane swiveled back and forth in her seat. "I guess Pump was right. I haven't been listening to him. Sometimes he gets these paranoid notions, and nothing comes of it." She gasped. "He says this will all be burned to the ground by the end of the month." Her voice hovered between wonder and horror.

Jim didn't know what to say. He stopped them at the line for the ferry and set the brake. On the other side of the river, oxen dragged their loads behind them up the Atascosito Road and toward the United States.

Jane craned her neck to see who was in front of them. "Peter!" she cried after releasing a relieved breath. "I'll be right back." She hopped down from the buckboard and hurried to reunite with her son.

This was good. They could travel together, Jim thought, but he had misgivings when he scanned Peter's team. Her son's oxen could only make ten miles a day to Jim's thirty with the horses. He counted the wagons in front of them and peeked behind. No one else had penned them in yet, but he could see another cart coming down the road.

When he turned back to face the wait, he recognized a Tonkawa man idling on the boardwalk. Jim's skin crawled. What a difference space and time made, he thought. It was only days ago that Mopai had scalped the trespasser, but Jim couldn't touch this man. He tore his eyes away before the Tonkawa noticed him staring. So strange that something so right at home could be so wrong here.

"I thought that was you."

Jim twisted and saw a man with a rifle cradled in his arm. He tried to recall the man's name. Was it Charles? "Morning."

The man walked away without responding, and Jim resisted an urge to roll his eyes like Eva. Anxious to move, he left the buckboard to wait with Jane and Peter.

When he approached, Peter greeted him with a handshake. Jim didn't know him very well. Jane's son had his own farm and family in another part of the colony. Though his memories of him as a boy, before they came to Texas, were fond ones, he had met him only a handful of times as an adult. In a parallel world, they would have remained close childhood friends through manhood.

"We can't leave soon enough, as far as I'm concerned," Peter said. "I'm betting Houston wants all our wagons. All those who aren't taking this seriously are going to end up on foot when Santa Anna comes." He turned his head to his mother. "I should have listened to Father sooner. You know how he is, though."

As they talked, Peter's face shifted to puzzlement at something over Jim's shoulder. Jim followed his gaze. Charles had returned with company. Jane's breath hitched, and Peter stepped forward to stand shoulder-to-shoulder with Jim.

"We didn't have any Comanche trouble until you came," the man said. "I don't know about you folks, but I'm not going to let this vermin waltz into our town without being challenged."

Jim skimmed the faces of the growing mob, his anxiety and anger rising in equal measure. When his eyes landed on the sneering Tonkawa, the organ in his chest flashed as if someone had thrown a handful of gunpowder on his hatred.

"Now you listen here, Charles Garret," Jane said. "I know on good authori—"

"Whose authority?" Charles asked. "Your husband's? Pumphrey Brunet's?" Charles spat. "You and everyone else here knows he has a blind spot for this boy. Why did he run away if he's not guilty?"

"Pump urged him to go because of hotheads like you," she said. "Jim knew nothing of the raid. Pump wouldn't entrust me to him if he didn't consider him an honorable man."

"I say we give like for like," a voice called. "I say we draw and quarter him. For Mrs. McMullen. And for being the traitor he is."

"Step aside, Mrs. Brunet," Charles said. "We should have done this ages ago." He scowled at Jim. "To think, we welcomed you." He spat again in disgust.

"Take his scalp while you're at it," someone from the back shouted.

Jim's eyes had never left the Tonkawa's. At the threat, the man's sneer slid to a satisfied grin, and he said, "Wait until after he's dead."

At those words, Jim's blood drained away, and his vision shifted to the other speakers. He darted his eyes from face to face, and time slowed. Peter moved in front of him to shield his body, and Jim crouched to run. Jane screamed at the men.

Three vigilantes tackled him and carried him mere paces away to a tall oak. Jim's mind blanked as his body took over. Sheer terror coursed through his veins. As they stripped his torso, he bucked against them and dodged as they pulled a noose over his head. When the rope tightened, the men released him.

Jim managed to get the tips of his fingers under the loop before it took his full weight. His toes pirouetted in the grass below him, and the vibrations of the rope groaned against his neck. He smelled smoke from a fire.

His body rotated away from the crowd, and Charles spun him back, knife in hand. Pressure built up behind his eye sockets and down his cheeks as if he had been hanging upside down for too long. The men's mouths moved, but he could no longer hear above the rushing in his ears, and his vision began to fade.

A skyward rifle shot reverberated against his chest. A moment later, someone cut the rope, and he dropped to the ground, his legs crumpling beneath him. His fingers struggled to pull the cord loose, but he felt himself losing consciousness. Someone else loosened the rope from his neck. Color flooded his vision, and his ears cleared. For a moment, his heart didn't beat right, like drummers no longer in sync, but then they found their rhythm again. He tried to swallow the pooled saliva in his mouth, but his throat wouldn't respond, and he let it fall into the dirt. Fire raged across the skin under his jaw.

Jane's hands stroked his head as if making sure it was still attached. Her hysterical cries blocked out the words of the men who were shouting above him. He trapped Jane's hands in his own and sat up. Cutting through the mind fog, he forced himself to focus.

Daniel Allen, the neighbor he had built a pen with months ago, stood over him with a rifle pointed at the mob. "This man helped me more than once. He may look and sound like an Indian, but he's Anglo inside. I don't believe he turned on his own people. I say, let him prove he's not a traitor. Tomorrow, I'm headed to join my brother-in-law, who's with the New Orleans Greys. They need every man. He'll go with me."

Jim stared up at Mr. Allen, a man as large and hairy as the bear that lived in the faraway, snowcapped mountains of his people's territory. The unsated mob grumbled.

"Daniel, you can't be serious," Charles said. "Remember what they did to Mrs. McMullen. To Tom."

"This man had no part in that. We need good fighters. I'll vouch for him."

When Charles made to argue, Daniel reseated the rifle on his shoulder and cocked it. "This ain't a discussion." He addressed the crowd, his gun still trained on the ringleader. "In case y'all've forgotten," he shouted, "Santa Anna is on his way. Remember Zacatecas? I suggest you get back to evacuating your families."

Those were the magic words needed to break the vengeful spell they had been under, and one by one, they drifted away. Jane helped Jim put his fringed buckskin shirt back on, and he rose without shaming himself to stand beside Daniel. As the crowd thinned, he saw Peter lying on the ground where the mob had overwhelmed and subdued him, his wife cradling his head in her lap and tears streaming down her face. Jane pushed through to reach his side. She sank next to him and pressed her ear to his chest. After a moment, she sat up with a tight, relieved smile and slapped at his cheeks.

"Go on," Daniel said to Charles.

Charles remained planted where he was, unable to accept defeat. Jim set a hand on the hilt of his knife but found it gone. When he swallowed, the flaming torch in his throat flared. Jim had never felt so vulnerable. He searched down the line of wagons for his horse and saw it and his belongings untouched.

Another man holding a musket approached, and Daniel nodded to him. The newcomer gripped Jim's knife by the blade and presented the handle to him. Jim tried to thank the man as he took it, but his voice wouldn't cooperate.

Charles spat a final time and shook his head at Daniel in disgust. "Shameful. Don't think we won't have words when you get back." As he turned away to retrieve his rifle from the ground, he sent Jim one last venomous glare. "I'll shoot you like a coyote and hang your carcass from my fence if I ever see you again."

Jim vowed to have the man's scalp on his pole.

When Daniel thumped a hand on Jim's shoulder, he flinched. Jim tried to speak, but Mr. Allen said, "Don't. Wait 'til tomorrow. We'll get you fixed up at home."

Jim nodded and cast his eyes meaningfully in Jane's direction. They walked together to the group still huddled where Peter had fallen. He had regained consciousness, and his wife was planting salty kisses across his battered forehead.

Jane peered up at him with red-rimmed eyes, then pushed herself to her feet to embrace him. "I'm so sorry, Jim. I'm so, so sorry."

Gently, he placed a hand on her back. He wasn't sure what she had to be sorry about. None of this had been her doing, and he was about to break his word to Pump.

"I have to leave you," he whispered.

She pulled him down to her ear, and he repeated himself, the pain greater than the first time.

"Yes, you must. I will be safe with my son. Pump will understand."

Jim dropped his eyes, guilt adding insult to injury.

When she hugged him to herself, the softness of her plump body comforted him, a distant echo from his childhood. She even smelled like his mother. For the first time since he had become a man, he wanted to cry until his heart emptied.

Abruptly, he backed away from her, brought her hands to his lips, and kissed them.

She stroked warm fingers down his cheek when he let go. "Be careful."

He inclined his head to her and then bent to shake Peter's hand. Though still bleary-eyed, Jane's son returned it with his own firm one. "Thank you," Jim mouthed.

Daniel was waiting for him, and Jim pointed to his horse. When they reached it, Jim retrieved his rifle and loaded it, putting his back to the river and Pump's buckboard. The weapon felt good in his hand.

As Jim packed the ball with excessive force, Daniel informed him of the rest of his errands and apologized for being unable to depart immediately. When he was ready, Jim led his horse, and they walked together into the heart of town. Jim remained outside at each stop, wary and with his back to the wall. With each passing moment, his terror subsided, but his belly burned. When he lifted his shirt to look, he realized he had not felt the first and only slice. Dried blood coated his stomach past his navel. To

Jim's relief, they left town twenty minutes later and returned to Daniel's farmstead.

As his wife Maggie stitched the shallow wound at the apex of Jim's ribcage and bathed his ravaged neck, a cold rage settled in Jim's heart. If he hadn't heard the town would be ashes in a matter of weeks, he'd burn it to the ground himself.

Chapter 2

Eva

Eva relaxed now that they were on the road and had a plan. Discovering what day it was had also helped. They had time. Time to find Tophe and stop him from killing Francisca Alavez. Time to convince him to run away from Lux Libera with her.

Pump rode stoically beside her. At his continued silence, Eva wondered if his thoughts were with Jane.

"Thank you for coming with me," she said, feeling guilty that she had pulled him away from his priority.

He gave a clipped nod, eyes unfocused.

As they walked, the steady clop of the horses' hooves, soothed her. "Do you support the revolution?" she asked, hoping to distract him.

Without turning to her, Pump said, "Santa Anna's become a tyrant. Even a lot of Tejanos and Mexicans, in general, feel the same. We just want the Constitution reinstated. Most Anglos don't want to split with Mexico, but he's left us no choice. His mandate to take no prisoners and give no quarter after battles, as if we're all pirates on the high seas, just confirms it."

Eva thought about the timelines where Santa Anna wasn't a cold-hearted dictator, as well as the Lux

Libera missions that forced him to become so. It made her profoundly sad.

"So, yes, you do?" she asked.

"Yes."

Eva decided to leave him alone. For the next hour, she watched the people passing them on the road heading northeast. Oxen plodded under light loads in hastily packed wagons. More families carried what they could on foot. She and Pump were the only ones riding southwest and often had to make way for the heavier traffic. By mutual agreement, they stopped to help a family repair a slipped axle on a buckboard.

When they halted for the night, Pump's attention returned to the world in front of him, and his mood improved. As they watered their ponies, he explained his new plans to move to Nacogdoches.

"Why haven't you left before now?" Eva asked. She removed her saddle from her horse and pulled a handful of grass to rub him down.

"All the people we came with from Tennessee live in Austin's Colony, as well as our sons. Plus, Nacogdoches has been a bit of a bandit's den. It's more civilized now." Pump placed his saddle next to hers, standing it on its pommel. "It's hard to look at bustling San Felipe and imagine there might be nothing left to come back to in May. I held out hope for a long time that those in power in this line would make different choices. Santa Anna, for one." He shook his head. "I regret I didn't warn more people, though. Jim was right."

Eva cleared an area for a small fire. "I think it's easier to see a disaster looming when you're not the one who's in the middle of it, even forewarned. Events unfold slower than people often realize, and people don't connect the dots until it's too late. And that's assuming they can even see the dots."

Pump tilted his head in acknowledgment as he brought her a pile of kindling. "True."

After she picked apart a strip of juniper ash bark, she rubbed it against itself, making a fluffy fire bundle. "I was thinking about your support of the revolution." As she sparked the flint against her steel, she paused, then blew softly, steadily until heavy white smoke bloomed and a tiny flame appeared. She placed it carefully in the tinder, and Pump joined her in breathing life into it, their heads low to the ground as if they were listening to the earth. When she sat back on her heels, she said, "I have a hard time caring about any particular outcome. I've seen so many, and people suffer in all of them."

"You just haven't ever seen the worlds where people get it right, and you don't care because you've never had to live with the results before."

"I still don't have to," she said, picturing her new life with Jim and the irrelevant outcome of the Texians' war. "At least not for several more decades." At darker thoughts, she added, "As long as we move to a different band." Ever-present and closer than she wanted to admit, the future weighed on her mind. "I've been thinking I should transport our entire village to a timeline where the plains are free and open, full of game with no invaders. I'm sure it exists somewhere."

"Would you be able to stop with just Jim's village? Don't they each have relatives in other bands? And family members other tribes have captured?" He scratched at the tuft of hair above his ears. "What about the people those captives have fallen in love with? Their entire tribes?" He took off his spectacles and cleaned them with his handkerchief. "And let's not forget the white men that native women have married, plus their white communities. Would you have a utopia or just move the problems that exist here to another place?"

Eva scowled, disliking him questioning her dream. She didn't have to take everyone. People could have a choice. Why couldn't it be successful and be one of those worlds that got it right? She laid another piece of kindling on the fire and changed the subject. "Speaking of living with results, I've been thinking more and more that I need to do something to stop Lux Libera, not just Tophe."

Pump dusted his knees and retrieved food. "Isn't it pointless to try to stop Lux Libera?" He passed Eva her parfleche.

"Maybe. But it shouldn't be up to one group of people to decide how others should live, what they choose. They're taking people's free will away." She dug in her bag.

"How would you go about stopping them?" Pump asked as he held out his hand for her empty water pouch, then walked in the direction of the spring they had camped near.

"I haven't figured that out yet," she shouted over her shoulder. "I'm hoping to have Tophe's help."

When Pump returned, he handed over her water, and she took a long drink. "What's Jim think of that?" he asked.

Eva wiped her mouth. "I haven't told him." At Pump's pursed lips, she added, "Yet."

Pump widened his eyes at her delayed revision. "A marriage built on secrets and lies won't be the kind of marriage you want in the long run."

"Oh?" she said around a bite of food. "Jane knows of all your traveling?"

"Jane doesn't know because she's never known. I'm gone, and I'm back the same instant, as far as she's concerned," he said, snapping his fingers. "And I'm never gone long enough to age. There's nothing for me to lie about." He unwrapped his own meal. "And… I'm not risking my life starting a war with Lux Libera. I'm just a tourist." He paused and looked at her with withering intensity. "You will be intentionally lying to a man who knows what you can do and cares if you are putting yourself in danger without his knowledge. If you don't manage to disappear without Lux Libera discovering you're a heretic, they're going to hunt you down. And you want to attract attention by moving an entire people to a different world?" He flicked the last layer of wrapping as if it were hot.

Eva felt her face turn stubborn, and she couldn't help it. Her head agreed with him, but her heart didn't. Lux Libera was her problem to solve, not Jim's; that world and this world were separate.

Pump eyed the set of her jaw and added, "If nothing else, you can't take chances with a baby you share together. It's wrong." After a moment, he stared into the fire. "And who's to say things don't go poorly, and Lux Libera sends people to execute Jim? You know as well as I do he's a dead man if they discover your relationship with him. Each child born to you will be a target."

Eva grimaced. Pump was right, especially considering her last heart-to-heart with Jim. Guilt pressed on her shoulders. In her mind, she had promised never to jump away from him during an argument, not to inform him of all traveling. He would never know, she had reasoned, and she had formed a loophole by pretending he used the terms interchangeably. Shame turned her stomach, and she held Jane's uneaten bread between light fingers.

"You're right," Eva said. When she sensed his eyes on her, she forced herself to return his gaze. "You're right, okay?" Hearing the petulance in her voice made her angrier.

"A marriage to an Anglo man living as a Comanche in 1836 is different than a Lux Libera partnership. I'm sure you've figured that out by now." His spectacles hung at the end of his nose, and he raised his eyebrows, waiting for her reply.

"Yes," she said through gritted teeth at his tone.

Pump smiled. "And I imagine Jim is having to adjust his expectations of you as well. Am I right?"

Eva twitched a shoulder but couldn't help returning his smile. "Yes." At his reminder that it wasn't only her who had to compromise, her feathers smoothed.

Pump pulled out his pipe. "Jim may be willing to go with you. Have you thought of that?"

"I know he would. Before we left the farm, he was constantly making me jump with him from place to place. I even took him to a different timeline once, trying to look for a waterpark, but since I did it blindly, we ended up on the edge of a volcano in some primordial time and nearly suffocated. He hasn't asked since."

Pump barked a laugh.

"Though in his defense, that was the day before his brother showed up with news of his father."

"Well, there you go," he said, as if that solved everything, and lit his pipe. "He sounds eager to me."

Did it solve everything? Eva studied Jim traveling with her from a new angle, as her partner as much as her husband. Her certainty remained that he would be uninterested in fighting a war with Lux Libera.

"Your experience with the volcano reminds me," Pump said. "I never did show you how to skim timelines."

Eva's ears perked. "That's right! I forgot you said you could do that."

"I could teach you now unless you're too tired from the day." Smoke billowed from his nose in two diaphanous streams.

"Now is better than the morning."

Pump clapped his hands together. "With everything that's been going on, I haven't traveled in a while. This will be a nice distraction from reality."

The novelty of his words jarred against her Lux Libera instincts, and Eva snickered to herself as she glanced at her outstretched fingers. Everyone was the center of their own real universe. When he stood, she followed.

After remembering the pipe in his hand, he set it next to the fire. They scanned the secluded area around them, but it was deserted. The refugees had camped closer to the road.

"Let's hold hands, and I'll do the traveling," he said. "That way, you can pay attention to what's happening. When I reach a line I want to preview, I'm going to open up about ten percent of my strings. It's like an eagle skimming the water. Just our talons are going to touch. We'll be able to feel without being pulled under."

Eva's heart pounded. Being able to preview a line would reveal the multiverse to her. She held out her hand to him, and he took it.

"Ready?" he asked, reminding her of Tophe.

"Always."

In the blink of an eye, Pump opened a portal with his free hand and stepped through, tugging her behind him. The sensation of having her loops closed for her was something akin to Jim pulling air from her lungs when they kissed. In the space between, she glimpsed the fabric of the universe. Symphonies of infinite particle strings worked in harmony as they passed over each thread. The bright notes of life, the dark tones of death — all of it cycled in an ever-complicating bolero of creation.

Pump opened a portion of her strings, and like nosy neighbors cracking blinds, the world below came into partial view. They were as ghosts.

Beneath her, she saw a city with modern skyscrapers and artificial forest towers, a version of Trondheim, Norway, in a warm world, judging by the signage. He closed her loops for her again and skimmed along the fourth dimension of the line.

When he opened them, the skyscrapers were gone, but the city was still there as a sprawling town hugging closer to the shrunken sea. A brown haze drifted above the buildings and palisades. Longships lined the dark gray water of the harbor, and white emerald mountains rose from the depths to block the sun. Snow lay thick on the ground, and across the roads and paths, people were skiing and traveling in horse-drawn sleighs.

He closed her loops again, and they skimmed through space farther north until they came to a camp surrounded by herds of reindeer. Though shorter and rounder, the skin-covered cones reminded her of Jim's village.

Pump opened all her loops, and Eva found herself hidden within the forest bordering the camp. As the sun peeked over the mountain at their back, they watched the people going about their day. These were like her ancestors in her childhood timeline. She remembered seeing a photo of a Sami man who looked exactly like her lost father when he was young, the father who was real, after all, inhabiting a slice of spacetime somewhere in the multiverse.

At the painful, bittersweet memory, she shivered, wishing she had her buffalo robe, and thought of the Norse living along the coast with their own captives from whom she was also descended, her existence a product of both love or force, incompatible worldviews morphing over the centuries, one giving way to another and back again.

When Pump turned his head to smile at her, he pointed at her mouth and whispered, "Your lips are blue." He retook her hand, and they followed his tether back to their campsite and the moment they had left.

Eva's spirits soared, and she beamed at her mentor. "This also means I don't have to jump from horizon to horizon!"

"Yes, but you'll need a lot of practice," he said, tempering her enthusiasm. "Until then, you may have to stick with jumping shorter distances, especially if you're tired."

Another valuable skill Lux Libera had hidden from their followers, she thought. Eva shook her head in frustration.

"Now it's your turn," Pump said.

Chapter 3

Jim

It took two days for Jim to swallow without pain. Daniel winced at Jim's swollen neck each time he looked at him. In an apparent effort to fill the silence, his rescuer talked for them both. Jim learned about the birth, life, and death of every Allen relation near and far. The one thing Daniel didn't tell him was where they were going.

The first day, Jim didn't care. Within the armor of his fury, the only thought he had produced in his own mind was that they were heading southwest in Eva's footsteps. Jim let his horse carry him and his friend think for him. He ignored the wagonloads of refugees clogging their way. That night, he fought the noose any time he closed his eyes, just as he had the previous one.

The second day, Jim noticed that when Daniel laughed at his own jokes, his chest and belly jiggled like the gelatin Mrs. McMullen had served him once. Jim glanced down at the man's horse and pitied the animal. It wasn't so much that Daniel was fat as just large in all dimensions. A massive brown beard covered all but his eyes and the tops of his cheeks. Back at the cabin, Daniel had nuzzled his giggling wife Maggie with it when they'd assumed Jim was asleep.

The morning they left, Daniel and Jim had escorted her to a neighbor's house. She and their small children were to travel with a caravan to safety. Though Jim witnessed the woman's tears, they hadn't touched him. He turned away to give them privacy, wanting his own wife.

The farther south they traveled, the more refugees they found traveling on foot. Their immigrant buckboards had long since been dismantled and made into tables and benches. Anglo and Tejana women struggled to pull carts by hand, their men nowhere to be seen. One cluster possessed only the clothes on their backs. A child sat in the mud, crying and refusing to move another step. From what Eva had told him, Jim imagined their breakfasts laying out on plates back home and uneaten, front doors standing unlatched and banging in the wind, and animals bellowing in their pens.

For those who did have wagons, a gang of men worked in tandem, preying on their fears, galloping past, and exhorting the people to flee faster. "The Mexican army has been sighted!" "Make haste!" "Lighten your loads!" Their comrades gathered up the valuables discarded along the roadside.

Typical, Jim thought, as he watched with bitter eyes.

After that, Daniel warned each group they passed.

By the evening of the second day, Jim could have talked but didn't want to. He curled up in his buffalo robe, back to the fire, and finally slept. In the morning, his head was clear. He scrubbed his teeth with a stalk of rough horsetail he found growing by the creek, rinsed, and felt like a new man, if a bit raw. For a moment, he imagined his bleeding heart in his hand and a sinew in his mouth with which to bind and harden it, but he set them aside at his next thought of Eva. He didn't want to live that way anymore.

The first thing he said when he returned to their camp was, "Thank you."

Caught off-guard, Daniel's hands froze on his half-rolled blankets, but he broke into a grin. "Hey! Your voice is back."

"I owe you my life."

Under his intense gaze, the man squirmed, so Jim dropped his eyes.

"You're a good man," Daniel said. "The world would be a little worse if they had lynched you. I hope another man would do the same for me."

The moment stretched as Jim pondered the ground, neither of them sure what to say next. Temptation held the door open for him to leave and find Eva. All he had to do was say farewell. As much as he liked Daniel, he didn't want to be in his debt.

"Ready to ride?" Daniel asked.

"Where are we headed?"

Daniel's brow creased. "Didn't I tell you?"

Jim shook his head and smiled. "I caught something about joining the Greys." The heavy memory pulled at the corners of his mouth.

"We're headed to Goliad to find my brother-in-law. His fool head joined up under the romantic notion that he's fighting for our liberty and equality." He tied the last of his gear to his horse. "Maggie's been after me since he entered Tejas y Coahuila with them folks — the New Orleans Greys — to go protect him. I couldn't say no to her any longer after Santa Anna made good on the Tornel Decree at the Alamo."

"You don't support the revolution?" Jim settled himself on his pony.

"No. Most Anglos don't. Most Tejanos certainly don't, though they have their revolutionaries, too. Why in the world would we want to risk life and property? For what? You know how hard we've worked to scratch out our livings in this colony. For the most part, Mexico leaves us alone. I'm content to be a Mexican citizen. It's the cotton farmers what started it all, demanding to be able to keep their slaves."

After pulling his last tie fast, Daniel mounted. "And we've got all these folks from the U.S. coming from all these southern states, stirring up trouble." He spat to the side, and they clicked their horses to a trot. "Now, I have to go play nursemaid to my wife's brother Will and hope I don't get caught doing it."

He pointed his finger at Jim. "Our first job is to convince Will to go back with us and evacuate like everyone else." He let his hand fall and added, "Of course, I imagine, you'll want to go your separate way when we reach Goliad."

Pleased to be able to provide a finite service for Daniel and unafraid of the dangers that might be ahead, relief loosened Jim's grip on his horse's mecate.

"I will be your right hand until you are on the road home with your brother-in-law." He tried not to think of Eva. "After that, I will answer your call whenever you need help."

Daniel's eyes widened, and he inclined his head. "Much obliged. Thank you." A moment later, he chuckled. "Assuming I can find you."

"Yes." Jim grinned. "Assuming you can find me. But I mean it, nonetheless. We don't know what the future will bring. I may be able to help you again someday."

Late afternoon found them outside the gates of the Goliad presidio. Hearty cheers went up when sentries announced the purpose of their arrival, and a man ran down the parade ground to embrace Daniel in a wild hug. Will, quite young and barely a man, wore a gray jacket with matching pants and a sealskin cap. Jim scanned the "men" going about their tasks; most had the scraggly whiskers of teenagers — all mere boys.

Daniel introduced Jim, and Will looked him up and down, obviously unsure what to make of his long hair and Nʉmʉ clothing. "Pleased to meet you," he said, presenting his hand for Jim to shake. Formalities concluded, Will led them on a search for the Quartermaster, eventually tracking him down in a storage room.

"Sir, new recruits," he said. "This is Quartermaster Holt," he added under his breath.

The Quartermaster held up a finger without looking up. After a moment, he jotted down a number and then raised his head. His gaze traveled from Jim to Daniel and back. "Names?"

"Rob Parker," Daniel said. Will's head swiveled in surprise. The man marked it down.

"James McCullough," Jim said, equally shocked by Daniel's answer. It would never have crossed Jim's mind to give a false name, and his integrity rebelled at the notion without further thought. Enlisting meant nothing to him. He was only here for Daniel.

"There might still be room on the floor in the barracks or in one of the tents around the parade ground. Just find a free spot." The Quartermaster slid his eyes to Will. "Make sure they don't pick any of Ward's or King's beds." To Jim and Daniel, he said, "Colonel Fannin sent their groups to rescue some families from Refugio, who waited too long to evacuate." He shook his head, sighing. "There's been no word from the men, though Fannin has sent messengers. They should be back any moment." With an apologetic frown, he scratched his head. "I don't have any other supplies I can give you besides a bed. Conserving for the upcoming siege. You'll be fed at mealtimes with the rest of the men. Did you bring your own firearms?"

They both nodded.

"Good. Have you been to see the paymaster?"

"Not yet," Daniel said.

"Pay is $20 a month. You stick with us a year, you get 1,280 acres, 960 for nine months, 640 for six, and 320 for three."

Every muscle in Jim's body tightened. These boys weren't here to fight for liberty. They were here to plunder land and have a little adventure on the side. He peeked over his shoulder at the full garrison and pictured all the other unofficial, unsanctioned militias of U.S. citizens that must be scattered across the territory. All those new acres wouldn't be given out from existing colonies.

"'Course, no one's getting paid right now, but there's no reason to think we won't get paid soon," the Quartermaster said.

Indifferent, Daniel lifted a shoulder.

"Did you ride or walk here?" the Quartermaster asked, looking at their feet.

"Rode," Jim said.

At this news, the Quartermaster's eyes lit up. "Excellent! I'll be requisitioning your horses for Horton's men. They need spare mounts."

"Whoa," Daniel said, the tops of his cheeks flushing red. "No one is requisitioning my horse."

"Don't worry. You'll get paid its worth when you get your enlistment pay. I keep impeccable records."

"You may not have my horse," Jim said.

The Quartermaster squared his shoulders and stared down his nose at him. "It's not up to you, son. Your horse is the garrison's now." He lifted his chin to one of the soldiers standing by, and the boy took off at a run to make it so.

"We want to join Horton's men, then," Jim said, eyes following the soldier.

Daniel took a step toward the Quartermaster and then, seeming to change his mind, pivoted in the direction of his horse. He brought himself under control a moment later and jerked his thumb at Jim. "What he said."

"I'm sorry, fellas," the Quartermaster said. "Horton's Mounted Rangers are excellent horsemen and a cohesive unit. They're not engaging new recruits right now." His focus darted between Jim and Daniel. "We need more infantrymen. And that's what the San Antonio Greys are."

Jim scoffed. "I guarantee you I can out-ride and out-shoot every single one of them."

"Maybe so," the Quartermaster said, smirking, "but I have my orders. Every new horse that passes through our gates is being requisitioned. Now, good day, fellas. I need to get back to work. The private here can show you the barracks and introduce you to your officers."

When the man turned his back on them, Jim's mouth fell open, and he nearly choked on his pride. Daniel pulled on his sleeve. Only the thought of stealing all the horses whenever he left persuaded Jim to walk away.

Out of earshot, Will rounded on Daniel. "Rob Parker? Who the hell is that?" His eyes and mouth shifted between amusement and disapproval.

"Seemed like a good idea in the moment," he said. "*San Antonio* Greys?"

Will shrugged in return. "We got reorganized. The politicians seemed to think we needed to be named after a Tejas town instead of New Orleans. Nobody really calls us that except Holt."

They found their gear and tack in a neat pile near the gate and followed Will to the barracks. The sleeping quarters were quiet and deserted. Jim checked his bags to make sure nothing had been stolen before stowing it all in an out-of-the-way corner. They'd sort out the sleeping situation that night. He didn't really care.

As they left the barracks and entered the parade ground, the volunteers were gathering in the open space. Will introduced them to each boy they met, one after another. Eventually, the new names ran together in Jim's head. He'd never be able to remember them all.

In the center, an older man held up his arms, calling out orders before the assembled garrison.

"That's Sergeant Major Rose, one of Fannin's officers," Will said, leading them to the crowd's edge. "We only listen to him if one of our own officers tells us to."

"You have different leaders?" Jim gazed around at the hodgepodge of threadbare uniforms and ragged Anglo clothing. Some of the men didn't even have shoes. He guessed it wasn't that different than Nʉmʉnʉʉ raiding parties coming together under different leaders for larger campaigns deep in Mexico. Still, he had assumed the Anglos would be more organized.

"We're volunteers, not the army," Will said. "We follow our own leaders. Good thing, too."

A sharp outcry drowned out the rest of Will's words, and the men in gray uniforms scowled and clenched their fists.

"We've spent weeks, more than a month...," one man shouted. "God, I lose track... a long damn time demolishing the outbuildings, burning the brush, and rebuilding the walls of this goddamn derelict fort." The man's face reddened with each word.

"That's Bill Hunter," Will said out of the side of his mouth.

The Sergeant Major opened his lips to speak, but Hunter continued, "If I had wanted to do back-breaking work instead of fighting Mexicans, I would have stayed home in Virginia." He shifted forward, hands on his hips. "Houston's orders to retreat to Victoria came days ago. Fannin decides to leave now? When the enemy may be close?" He peered around at his fellow Greys and pointed to the ground. "Fort Goliad will withstand anything Mexico throws at us. Am I right, boys?"

A roar went up from the Greys, Will included. The other men in different militias darted glances at each other and their officers.

"Captain Pettus, control your men," Rose bellowed.

The man he addressed stood nearby with his arms crossed. He shrugged and replied, "I'm inclined to agree with them, as you know."

Rose inhaled from his toes.

In answer, Pettus rolled his neck and unfolded his arms. "Boys," he said, raising his voice, "We've been outvoted. Again. Unless we want to be the only ones defending Fort Goliad, we're headed to Victoria. Best not to leave the cannons for Santa Anna."

Moans rose like a cloud from the disaffected soldiers. The Sergeant Major ignored them and snapped to action, identifying cannons to bury and hurling commands. His voice increased in volume over the complaining. Nine artillery pieces needed to be hauled down from atop the bastions and interred in the parade ground. The rest would travel with them. Jim joined the group sent to retrieve a six-pounder.

"Damn Fannin," a boy said, running up to Will. He cast his eyes over Daniel and Jim as they strode to the fort's northeast corner, and Will made the introduction. "This is Noah Dickenson. He's from Canada."

Jim's eyebrows rose at the thought of Canadians joining the land grab. To cover his surprise, he asked, "Why did Rose call this Fort Defiance when we first walked up?"

Will and Noah snorted. "Because Fannin decided it was a good use of his time to rename the fort. He came up with three options and then drew from a lottery. We're pretty sure he rigged it to pick his favorite: Fort Defiance. It'll only ever be Fort Goliad to us Greys."

Chapter 4

Eva

After three days on the road, Eva rejoiced to see the embankments of El Copano. The Texians had fortified the safest and deepest port on the coast before the Mexicans had regained it mere weeks ago, though it still amounted to little more than a warehouse and freshwater cistern with rows of tents. It would be several more years before a frontier trading post, Corpus Christi, would appear thirty miles farther down the beach, eventually becoming one of the United States' largest ports.

Eva had told Pump to pack extra water pouches, and they filled them before they crossed the last stream. Fresh water was unreliable at this site, and it had only ever been a smugglers' hole until Irish immigrants began landing there on their way to San Patricio. The Mexican government had no desire for Anglos to establish a permanent town in such a strategic, if chronically dry, location.

The smell of salt and seaweed blew toward them through the huisache and mesquite, and the arcing, wind-blown oak trees reminded her of Tophe slicking back his black hair. She brushed her own out of her eyes, her coiled braids having come unpinned in the stiff coastal breeze.

"Do you know any Spanish?" Eva asked.

Pump wobbled his head. "Some, from trading with Tejanos and Comanches. I can understand more than I can speak."

"That's better than nothing." Eva puckered her lips for a moment. "Okay, this is what we're going to do. You're my Anglo father I have fetched because of the revolution. You're a loyal Mexican citizen seeking shelter with your daughter and her officer husband. Got it?"

"Did you travel alone?" Pump asked.

"No. My escort defected to join the Texian cause. I am shocked and scandalized." She fluttered an ironic hand on her breast. "Luckily, I reached my father safely before the man deserted me."

Pump chuckled, clearly impressed.

Eva flicked both brows up and smiled back before nudging her horse forward. When they approached the guards, she knew them both and resisted the urge to call them by name. They had never met her before in this world.

"Good day, sirs," she said in Spanish.

The guard on her right, squinting in the sun, shielded his eyes as he looked up at her. "Good day, madam." While she explained their situation, his gaze traveled over her and Pump. At the name "Lieutenant Benavides," he tipped his hat and welcomed them to enter.

In confusion, Eva blinked at the guard but then recovered with a dip of her head. She'd planned to explain that her husband would arrive with the coming reinforcements in the next few days. He shouldn't recognize Tophe's cover name yet.

Pump dismounted and joined her on foot, and she led them through the camp to the spot where servants always set up their tent. In place of empty ground, she found one sitting there, already pitched. She stepped toward it but backed away, touching her forehead.

"What's wrong?" Pump asked.

"This isn't supposed to be here yet. Tophe isn't supposed to be here yet." She bent at the waist to peer into the tent but didn't see anyone. "I don't even know if that's actually our tent or not."

"Eva!"

At the sound of Tophe's voice, she turned. He jogged toward her down the main avenue, and her heart sang. Enlisted men saluted him as he passed. When he reached her, he caught her up in a fierce hug, and she buried her face in his neck. She never wanted to let go again.

"Where have you been?" He seemed to notice Pump staring and dropped his hands. Before Tophe cleared his features, Eva read the question in his eyes.

"I'll stake the horses," Pump said in English.

"Is this our tent?" Eva asked.

Tophe furrowed his brow as he followed her finger. "Yes, of course."

Abruptly, she took his hand and pulled him inside.

"Who was that?" he asked, then scanned her up and down. "And what are you wearing?" He grasped her chin and tilted it to the side. "Look at your hair! How long have you been here?"

"Ah," she said, holding up a finger. "That's the question. I've been here six or seven months."

Tophe's jaw dropped open. "And I thought *I* was here early." He gave a low whistle. "You went to the other beacon."

"Yes. You saw it too, then?" Overwhelmed with relief that he had seen the same thing, she hugged him to herself until he released the air in his lungs.

"The scouts are getting sloppy," he wheezed. Tophe wrapped his arms around Eva and tapped out. "I need to breathe." With a tug of his hands on her elbows, he sat her on one of the cots. "Okay, who's that?" he asked, jerking his thumb over his shoulder.

"That's your father-in-law, but really, he's a friend who helped me return to you."

Tophe's face clouded. "What do you mean a 'friend?'"

"Señor?" a voice called from outside the tent.

At the interruption, Tophe cursed under his breath. "Uno momento, por favor," he shouted. To Eva, he said, "I just came back here to get something." He grimaced. "I've actually had to do real officer work. Give me a couple of hours, and then we can talk."

Eva followed him out, and Tophe introduced her to Private Gonzales, his clerk.

"Madam Benavides," the man said with a nod. His handsome mestizo face reminded her of Miguel. Gonzales would rise to be a powerful Mexican officer one day, something he'd never be able to do in this line's American army.

As she took his hand, she wondered how the slave-holding, Indian-hating Texians could claim they were fighting to establish liberty for all. They disdained Mexico's "old world aristocracy" as a barbaric and unfair caste system while their own Anglo society operated completely contrary to their stated ideals. But then, the answer hit her with sudden clarity, chilling in its simplicity. Rather than betray their principles, they simply considered non-whites subhuman, and if they weren't humans, they couldn't be citizens. Et voilà! Everyone's equal if you limit the guest list.

Tophe kissed her on the cheek in farewell, and Eva shaded her eyes as she watched them stride away to the warehouse where the officers administered the camp. The military village of tents was much as she remembered it, just a few days too soon. In the distance, Pump struggled toward her with their gear, and she hurried to help him.

When Tophe returned, he secured a separate tent for Pump, and then they dined with the other officers and their wives. Eva told their story, and the women gasped at her abandonment by her escort.

"Well, you're here now and safe," Colonel Vara, the ranking officer of El Copano, said. "I would have expected such treacherous treatment from a Norteamericano, but it's hard to imagine a Mexican doing such a thing." He darted his eyes at Pump. "No offense to your father, of course, madam."

Eva waved her hand. "No offense taken, I assure you. He's of the same opinion. He has long since converted to the one true church and been less and less welcome in his community. I've been trying, for years, to convince him to move to Mexico City and live with us."

Pump's jaw ticked as he concentrated on his plate. When he looked up, the glare he shot her poked an invisible hole between her eyes, and she coughed.

"That's something I've never understood," Madam Vara, the Colonel's wife, said. "The Norteamericano settlers promised to convert to Catholicism, yet they are still heretics, as far as I am aware, with their own churches and schools. They pay more attention to the United States than their own country, and they refuse to speak Spanish! If you ask me, we've let them govern themselves far too long, and now we're paying for it."

The captain sitting next to Eva wiped his mouth. "At least the gringos are a buffer between us and the Comanches. Let them be the ones to bleed while the land is settled. They can wipe each other out as far as I'm concerned."

As Tophe scraped together the last bite from his plate, he stared at her as if he wished they were telepathically linked. If he wasn't focused on her, he was studying Pump or uncharacteristically asking someone to repeat themselves as the table jiggled with his leg. She kicked him to make him stop.

When Colonel Vara stood to signal the end of the meal, Tophe said, "Rather than join you this evening, sirs, I'd like to help my wife get unpacked."

Eva gazed lovingly up at him, and Pump frowned. The other officers shared a knowing smile and waved them off.

As she walked between them on their way back, Pump kept twisting around and looking behind them. Tophe said nothing. When they reached Pump's tent and Eva bid him goodnight, the corners of Pump's cold mouth lifted without a glance in their direction, then he pushed back the flap and disappeared inside.

Tophe took her arm and placed it in his. "Let's walk where no one can overhear us."

As they strolled, Eva laid her head on his shoulder, and tears came to her eyes. Every muscle in her body relaxed, and an incredible, unexpected longing for the sanctum flooded her.

Tophe peeked down at her in surprise.

"I just missed you so much."

"Wish I could say the same," he said with a laugh. "It's only been a few days for me."

She resisted the unladylike urge to punch him and settled for pinching the inside of his arm.

He yelped. "I definitely didn't miss that, Eva." He pinched her back and twisted.

"Truce!" she said, cringing away.

Tophe grinned in triumph. When they were suitably distant from eavesdroppers, he turned to her. "Okay, details please, ma crotte. I can't take the suspense anymore."

She told him of stepping out into darkness only to fall into the gully. "A man found me and nursed me back to health. He let me stay with him until now. Pump is a good friend of his." As she tucked her hair behind her ear, she focused on the horizon. "He couldn't leave the farm, so Pump agreed to escort me."

"That's it?" he asked.

"Yes, pretty much."

"What have you been doing this whole time?"

"Helping him with the farm."

"How old is he?"

"Our age."

"Does he have a wife?"

"No."

"And he didn't expect anything?"

"Nope."

Tophe pursed his lips and gave her a sidelong glance.

"Really. He was a perfect gentleman."

He stared down at her, searching her face. She kept her eyes steady.

"I'm surprised you didn't go back to the sanctum," he said.

"I would have, but the head injury messed with my ability to travel, and it took me months to get it back. By the time I healed, it made sense just to wait and meet up with you."

Tophe nodded and looked away. They could see the ocean from where they stood, and the setting sun skipped over the waves, leaving golden streamers.

Chapter 5

Jim

Presidio La Bahía Goliad

By the time the militias finished burying the cannons, the parade ground resembled a graveyard. "That's not going to fool any Mexicans," Noah, the Canadian, said. "We should've spiked them." At Jim's questioning face, he added, "You ram a hot piece of metal down the touchhole where the fuse goes. Only good for scrap after that."

As they lined up for the evening food rations, Daniel's brother-in-law, Will, took them through another lengthy round of introductions and names Jim would quickly forget. Joseph Spohn, a creole from Louisiana, slitted his dark eyes. "Finally… an Anglo settler is bothering to get his hands dirty in his own war for independence."

Daniel bristled, straightening his spine, but remained silent.

"He's here now," Will said. "That's all that matters."

Spohn huffed and crossed his arms. "Our men died at the Alamo for you. Where were you then?"

"Be angry with Fannin," Noah said. "Not these fellas."

"What did Colonel Fannin do?" Jim asked.

"He refused us provisions to reinforce our brothers. If we had been able to return to the Alamo, we could have turned the battle." Spohn's dark eyes sparked.

"When Fannin finally answered Travis' call, it was too late," Will added.

"Colonel West-Point-Drop-Out needs a consultation with his officers to wipe his own ass," Spohn said. They all stepped forward with the food line, and the men ahead and behind joined their conversation.

In front of them, a private from South Carolina twisted at the waist and stuck his thumbs in the band of his trousers. "Tell them about our rescue attempt."

A couple of the men smirked, but many scowled.

"Fannin finally… finally!" Spohn exclaimed, addressing the sky, "gathered up most of the garrison, including all of us, and headed out with wagons. We were crossing the San Antonio River — that one right there," he said, pointing to the north, "the one you can fucking see standing from the bastion — and not one, not two," he ticked off on his fingers, voice rising, "but three of our wagons broke down."

"We could have walked back to our own bunks," Will interjected, "but Fannin had us camp right there in the cold rain."

"We didn't have many experienced wagoners," Spohn said. "All of our previous ones had been Mexican, and they asked for discharges once the Declaration of Independence was signed. They had only been sticking with us while there was still a possibility of a separate state of Tejas within the Mexican confederation." He spat at the feet of an imaginary disloyal Tejano. "With them gone, nobody else thought to picket the oxen."

"So, all the animals wandered off by morning," Will said.

The Canadian, who had been quietly listening, covered his mouth, and tears leaked from the creases of his eyes, his body shuddering.

"I don't know how you can laugh, Noah," Spohn said.

Beet red in the face, the boy shook his head. After a breathless moment, he said, "I'm sorry. It's too funny. You gotta admit."

"People died because of those damn oxen," Spohn shouted.

"I know, I know." Noah put up placating hands and sobered as best he could.

"They died because of Fannin," Will said. "Fannin is the one who took a vote in the morning — without consulting the Greys — to abandon the men at the Alamo. The oxen didn't call for that vote. We found out about the decision when we started marching back."

At the memory, Noah stopped laughing. A pall fell over the group, and they took another step as the queue moved forward.

"If you think Fannin is such a bad leader, why do you follow him?" Jim scanned the ragged line of soldiers. "He sounds weak and unworthy."

The men and boys glanced at each other. "We wouldn't just desert," Noah said. "We're not cowards."

Will's voice dropped to a whisper. "But some are urging Pettus to mutiny."

The boys around him shifted their weight and peeked over their shoulders. Noah coughed and palmed the corners of his eyes.

That night, Daniel and Jim cornered Will away from the fires, the brandy drinking, and the music.

"I can't believe you're asking me to desert, Dan," Will hissed through his teeth. "What kind of a man do you take me for? I'm fighting for your liberty! Yours!"

Daniel pinched the bridge of his nose, then opened his hand and raised his head. "This isn't your fight. There's nothing you need to liberate me from. If anything, you're endangering me and mine — your own sister and nieces and nephews. The Mexicans have been welcoming to us, and they feel like the revolutionaries are stabbing them in the chest."

"When I have my land here," Will said, "I want it to be free, like the United States, with a constitution and a representative democracy. I don't want to be a slave to a dictator." Will darted his eyes at Jim. "What are you shaking your head at?"

"There's no land for new settlers," Jim said. "They'll be giving it to you out of Nʉmʉnʉʉ Sookobitʉ. The Mexicans call it Comanchería. It won't be a safe place to build or farm. You'll be at war with the Nʉmʉnʉʉ."

"Who are the Nʉmʉnʉʉ?" Will stumbled over the word.

"Comanches," Daniel said.

"So what? I can lick any Indian."

Disgusted, Jim pulled the mask over his features and took a step back, but seeing Daniel's frustrated and agonized face, he calmed himself and tried another approach. "It's stupid to follow a leader who clearly doesn't know what he's doing. My people only follow men who have proven themselves over and over again. If I disagree with a war leader, I just leave. If I have given a leader my trust, I obey him immediately and without question. Whatever's going on here is going to get a lot of men killed."

"Who are your people?"

"The Nʉmʉnʉʉ," Jim said. "The people you think you can so easily lick." Jim enjoyed the embarrassment that swept over the boy's face. It didn't last long.

"I've heard Indians never hold their ground or stay and fight." Will's arrogant nose lifted as he peered over it at Jim.

"Why stay when you're outnumbered? It's not smart. We live to fight another day." Jim gestured at the ten-foot-high and three-foot-thick walls surrounding them. "We certainly don't die for a building." He felt his lip curling and straightened it out. Studying Will's face, he saw he was having no impact. If anything, they were strengthening the boy's resolve. His voice rose. "Half your fighters aren't even men yet. They're just boys pretending to be."

Will's jaw ticked as he drew himself up to his full height. "I won't abandon my brothers." He turned on his heel and threw his final words over his shoulder. "You can desert if you want, but I'm staying here."

Jim set his hands on his hips. Those loyal words were the first Jim could sympathize with. He shared a long look with Daniel until the other man shook his head.

"It's hard for Will to see past the acreage he'll earn in this war."

"Only Anglos use land as money," Jim said. "It's stupid."

"When you're judged a man by how many acres you possess, it's hard not to." Daniel exhaled and ran his fingers through the bottom of his beard. "Replace horses for land, mix it with adventure and battle-won glories, and I think you'll understand it's an irresistible opportunity for any American boy wanting to be counted among men."

Jim grimaced as his assessment hit home.

"I guess we're revolutionaries now," Daniel said.

Panic gripped Jim's heart and squeezed. "We could just bind him and cart him off. That works, too."

Daniel laughed and clapped him on the shoulder.

"I'm not joking."

His friend's only answer was to sigh and nod. "I know."

The following morning, a rider galloped into the presidio and closeted himself with Fannin and his staff. Within twenty minutes, the rumors circulated about people Jim knew nothing about and cared even less. King and his men — those previously sent to rescue refugees — had been caught and executed. Ward, who had been belatedly sent to help King, was on the run with his soldiers somewhere in the wilderness, and five hundred Mexican soldados had been spotted a short distance away. Before another ten minutes passed, the whispered undercurrent turned into hard orders to dig up the cannons and prepare to defend Fort Defiance.

Jim stared in disbelief at the men scrambling around him. After several beats, he picked up a shovel with all the urgency of a condemned man. Heavy smoke billowed over the walls as the volunteers torched the last few outbuildings. In the next moment, Fannin ordered the men to prepare to depart.

"Which are we doing? Staying or going?" Will asked.

"Bugger me if I know," Noah, the Canadian, said. "Both, it sounds like. Right now, I have a shovel in my hands, and I'm digging up a cannon. That's as much as I can tell you."

Will groaned.

"I'll feel better when these are back up on the bastions, though. That's for damn sure," Noah said.

"Did you hear Houston ordered to blow up the fort before we leave?" Will pitched his dirt onto the growing pile.

"Like hell I will," Noah said. "Besides, can you imagine the quantity of firepower we would need to do that? Last I checked, we didn't get a shipment of all the fucking explosives in Tejas y Coahuila."

Will speared his shovel into the mound and jumped down into the hole. "At least we didn't spike the damn things."

"It's harebrained to abandon the strongest fortress in Texas." Noah thrust his hand toward the storerooms. "We have provisions for six weeks, for cryin' out loud."

Jim pictured himself trapped between these walls until the summer months, and he shuddered.

"You just gonna watch, or you gonna help?" Will asked Jim.

"Sorry." Jim dropped into the other end and bent to lift the cannon.

Preparing for two different options at the same time, suffering an attack or sneaking off in retreat to Victoria, took all night. In the earliest hours of the morning, men hitched the oxen to the wagons, and a brigade formed to pass crates and baskets from the storerooms to the beds of the buckboards. Someone tied Jim's own horse to one of the smaller carts. All the while, a chilly rain fell, and though the walls blocked the brisk north wind, the men shivered and complained.

Jim packed, hauled, and eyed his horse, but his conscience echoed in his head with every footfall.

You can't abandon Daniel. He saved your life. You gave your word.

His thoughts drifted to Eva. She should be in El Copano, but she had always said the "Angel of Goliad." He kicked himself for not demanding full details. When he was free of his obligation to Daniel, he didn't know if he should go toward the coast, stay here and wait for her, or make his way to Pump's relatives.

At some point during the night, Jim sheltered in a pile of lumber behind the chapel and went to sleep.

Chapter 6

Eva

El Copano

Pump and Eva idled away the afternoon. Francisca Alavez, the future Angel of Goliad, wouldn't arrive until the next day with the reinforcing regiment, the same day she and Tophe were originally supposed to travel and blend in with the camp.

"So, what's your plan here?" Pump asked. They sat on a beach, far from the tents. When she hesitated, he added, "You seem to have fallen into your former life with ease."

At his tone, she swung her head to face him.

He gazed straight ahead at the waves, disapproval in the line of his lips.

"I'm still figuring that out. I couldn't very well just come out and tell Tophe everything. Not immediately."

"You're very convincing as his wife, by the way."

As she searched his profile, her lips parted. "What do you mean by that, Pump?"

"I saw the way you looked at him, Eva." The eyes he turned to her could have burned a hole. "Be very glad you brought me instead of Jim."

She shot to her feet, scattering sand from her skirts. "What the hell, Pump?"

He stared up at her, jaw hardening, before he returned his focus to the ocean, clearly disgusted with her.

"Celibacy, remember? It's an act. He's like my brother. Closer than a brother." Her stomach clenched around a ball of nausea at the thought of being intimate with him, and she scrunched her nose. "Do I care for him? *Yes*. Like a *brother*."

"Then let this serve as a warning. You should never put on that 'act' in front of Jim."

Her mouth gaped until she clamped it shut. "How dare you!" she said, her feet sinking into the sand as she stomped away.

"The lady doth protest too much, methinks," Pump shouted after her.

Eva whipped around and strode back. "Fuck you." She wanted to kick sand in his lap but settled for jabbing her finger in his face. He leaned back from it; then, she turned on her heel to trod through the dune. He called after her, but she ignored him.

Up on the grass, she passed another man and woman on their way to the beach. They trailed her with their eyes, strangely intense, and she bobbed her head at them. Instantly, she realized her face might be fierce and tried to smile. Strange, she thought. They hadn't been at the officers' evening meal the night before. They must be camp followers. Something about how they had studied her unnerved her, and she peeked back at them, but they ambled on their way, their heads together like lovers.

When she reached the cavalry training ground, she stopped. A warm sun streamed through the clouds, but the wind continued to cut. She stood near a tree, avoiding its shade, and wrapped a blanket around herself. The soles of her boots had collected a gritty layer of sand and mud. As she pretended to watch the riders, she only saw Pump's indignant face. Her cheeks burned. She told herself she had done nothing wrong.

With lances lowered, the horsemen galloped as one across the clearing. She tracked them with her eyes as they did a coordinated spin. Moments later, Eva heard footsteps behind her. She wouldn't give him the satisfaction of noticing him.

The apology she expected didn't come. When she gave in to curiosity, no one was there, and the hairs on the back of her neck rose. She had been sure Pump had walked up behind her, but he trudged down the path in the distance, eyes glued to his feet.

"I believe I owe you an apology," he said when he reached her.

"You think?"

He winced. "I'm sorry."

She wasn't ready to forgive him. They stood in silence and watched the cavalrymen thrusting their lances through rings.

"Is there a part of you that wants to return to Lux Libera?" Pump asked. "Be honest."

The elegant horses of the Mexican cavalry pranced in formation. Eva never tired of watching them in any timeline. As she thought over her answer, her fist pulled the blanket tighter.

"Yes."

"Thank you for not lying to me." At her glare, he put up his hands. "I witnessed how easily lies rolled off your tongue yesterday."

Incensed, she turned her whole body to face him. "Look here, Pump. I don't need to defend myself to you," she said, pointing at the ground. "What you call lying, I call acting. There's often even a script, but Tophe and I work off each other. We're a team, improvising as we go." She poked her own chest. "When we're our real selves, we don't lie. I haven't lied to you since the day you called me out as a traveler."

"But you *are* lying to Tophe." His words punched her in the gut.

She crossed her arms over her belly. "Tophe is going to need to be eased in gently."

"You don't have a lot of time for that, honey."

Presidio La Bahía Goliad

"Where were you?" Daniel asked.

Jim jerked his head toward the northern wall. "Took a nap." The height of the morning sun surprised him. At least the rain had stopped.

"I'm not sure I could have gotten away with that." Daniel sounded envious as he scratched the back of his damp head and yawned like a lion. Prominent dark streaks ran under his bloodshot eyes.

From the bastions and roofs on the western wall, another cheer erupted. Jim thumped Daniel on the back, and they ascended the northwestern ramp in front of the chapel. Jim wedged his shoulder between two men and viewed Horton's Rangers chasing a small band of Mexican cavalry across the glen. The combatants exchanged shots, but no one fell. For the moment, the enemy took shelter in a line of trees, and Horton held his men out of range, safe and watchful.

Jim scanned the horizon. He didn't see five hundred soldados marching on them. Weren't they supposed to be leaving for Victoria? He glanced over his shoulder at the draft animals standing in their traces. What were the officers waiting for?

Laughter trickled through the audience. The Mexicans regrouped to form another charge against Horton's men. Jim watched little Herman Ehrenberg, a German boy who had been his neighbor in the brigade line, turn and haphazardly fire a pistol behind himself. The riders made it to the shelter of the next copse of trees, and the Mexicans halted in the middle of the prairie.

Jim roared with the rest of the volunteers when Horton's boys rallied and chased the enemy back across the field. Someone passed out brandy, and the atmosphere blossomed into a festival. Will pressed his hand down on Noah's shoulder, jumping and stabbing the air, excited to finally engage the enemy.

Several hours ticked by, and more than one man and boy were properly drunk before the sun shone overhead. Jim abstained with a tight smile and repeated wave of his hand. He hadn't grown up with alcohol since his capture, and the Nʉmʉnʉʉ refused strong spirits. With battle looming, drinking seemed particularly unwise. He didn't understand the choices they made.

His stomach growled, though, and that urge he did understand. The sudden combination of hunger and powerlessness transported him to his boyhood. The fort disappeared, and he stood once again before his master's chief wife.

Captives ate last, and during hard times, they went without. Wʉʔrabiahpʉ̱ knew he swiped food, but she could never figure out where he was putting it. She would make him stand in front of her and turn around with his arms out straight, moccasins off. One time she even patted his breechcloth, the only article of clothing he wore. She beat him after that and took him to Parʉhya Kuma̱.

Parʉhya Kuma̱'s eyes glittered. "Time to tell your secret, boy."

Unable to defy his master, Jim pulled a piece of dried meat from his matted hair and braced himself for death.

Parʉhya Kuma̱ doubled over with laughter, palm on the floor of the kahni. When he could talk, he told an annoyed Wʉʔrabiahpʉ̱ to give such a clever boy more to eat. To Jim, he said, with a toothy grin, "You will never starve."

The memory dissolved, and Jim's body pointed out that it would be a simple thing to steal whatever he wanted with everyone distracted. He was no ox stuck in its traces. Even the Quartermaster, his clerk, and the commissary officer held cups and toasted each other. He might not be a free man at the moment, but he'd be damned if he was ever helpless again.

Just as Jim descended to explore his breakfast-pilfering options, several men directed everyone's attention to the horizon. A line of Mexican infantrymen had appeared. The volunteers shouted a confused chorus of warnings, waving and gesticulating to those below. When Horton's men finally noticed the soldados, they tried to make a run for the fort, but it was too late. The combined enemy force cut them off.

The chase over the meadow began anew, but this time, Horton didn't stop. He continued onward to the San Antonio River. They urged their mounts across and took shelter in the nearby ruins of Mission Espíritu Santo, with the Mexican cavalry close behind them.

The watching men on the bastions and roofs raced to action. Captain Shackleton of the Red Rovers called for more volunteers, and Will shot his fist in the air. Daniel cut his eyes at Jim and raised his hand. Jim's own arm floated upward as if pulled by a string, then he shrugged. "Could be fun."

The corners of Daniel's mouth lifted at his friend's sarcasm before they ran to retrieve their weapons.

Returning to the parade ground, Jim didn't know what to make of the Red Rovers, yet another one of the six separate volunteer militias from the United States. The women of their Alabaman town had sewn them fringed shirts of red, green, and brown checks with red trousers to match. They were colorful, but he hoped they could fight better than most Anglos.

Will bounced from foot to foot, already sweating. Jim rested his rifle on his toe and waited. When all were prepared, they took off through the gates of the presidio at a jog. Jim searched the landscape but saw no other groups of enemy soldiers. Lone scouts hid in the trees.

At the river, they held their rifles and powder above their heads and waded through the chest-high, freezing water. The swollen current tugged at Jim's legs and sucked at his moccasins.

Jim's teeth chattered before he even emerged on the other side. After scrambling up the crumbling banks, their jog shifted into a run at level ground. Shackleton brought them to a halt out of range, and they regrouped to wait for stragglers. Jim hopped in place to stay warm. Others copied him without self-consciousness. The sun broke through the clouds, but a gust of wind covered it again a moment later.

"Right, boys," Shackleton said. "Let's line up over there where we can flank the Mexicans." He indicated the area, and the men nodded.

Positioned and ready to advance, they heard a resounding boom from the presidio, followed by another concussion. Mexican faces turned in the fort's direction; while at the same time, a ball hollowed the dirt between both forces. The second landed mere feet from Jim and showered him with mud and rocks. He ducked, protecting his head. If the range had been any shorter, it would have hit one of the Texians.

The Mexicans and Texians scattered in opposite directions.

"What are they goddamn thinking?" Shackleton shouted at everyone and no one as they ran.

A faint cheer drifted from the fortress, and Will threw his cap down in frustration. Daniel glanced at Jim, and Jim hid his unexpected disappointment. The thrill of the fight coursed through his veins, hard to douse once aroused without being spent.

Horton's men exited the ruins of the mission and rode ahead on tired horses. The Red Rovers and their leader groused the entire walk, wade, walk of the return journey. "We had every advantage there," Shackleton said. "We could have faced an even larger force and prevailed."

Suddenly, a rock nailed Jim's heel, and he checked behind him.

"Sorry," Will said. His muddy boots dragged along the ground, and he grimaced in apology. "I kicked it, and it didn't go where I expected it to."

Jim studied his own caked moccasins. Judging by the rotten state of some of the men's footwear, he didn't think the Quartermaster would have boots to give him for the march to Victoria. Regardless, they were probably stuck here, and Jim wouldn't need them anyway. With sudden dismay, he realized he was thinking in English and not his people's language.

Nothing else happened the rest of the day. The men waited for the order to evacuate, but it never came. Fannin paced the walls or met behind closed doors with his officers. A dark moonless night descended on the fort, and Fannin finally ordered men to ready the retreat. He sent Horton's Rangers out again to scout the way, but they returned with reports of enemy picket guards at each ford. Fannin rescinded the order and made another round of inspections.

Jim stood guard duty with a man named Abel Morgan from Kentucky. Morgan had escaped a wife who, in his words, had a turbulent disposition and made his life disagreeable, though the man himself was good-natured and affable. They watched Fannin meander toward them with Captain Westover of the regular army. One of the oxen bellowed below on the parade ground. Jim wondered if no one had thought to feed or water the draft animals since they had been hitched the night before. He hadn't seen any signs of it.

When Colonel Fannin reached their post, he asked Morgan, "What do you think about retreating?"

Captain Westover stood to the side with his hands clasped behind his back.

Morgan pushed his hat back and scratched his scalp. "Well, sir, I think it's a bit late, to be frank about it. We're well-surrounded now by the enemy, and we have about three hundred men and provisions for weeks. I think we can hold them off until Houston can come. We're in a much better situation than the Alamo was."

Captain Westover's face hid thinly veiled satisfaction. Fannin tucked his lips and ran his eyes over the artillery and the balls stacked in a nearby crate, calculating in his head. Jim imagined him scratching and erasing as he was unsure whether to add, subtract, multiply, or divide.

"I agree with you, Morgan," Captain Westover said. "If we had left three or four days ago, we might have escaped. But now..." He let the words hang, his eyes drilling into Fannin.

Fannin refocused on the men before him. "Thank you, soldier. Westover...," he said as he turned and strode back down the ramp. Captain Westover lifted his eyebrows at some internal thought of his own and followed.

"Bastard doesn't even know my name," Morgan said when the Colonel was out of earshot.

Rain pelted Jim and Morgan off and on all night. Miserable and cold, Jim abandoned his post and tracked down Daniel. Pump's words from the night Eva had revealed herself whispered in his ear.

"We need to go," Jim said. "We need to grab Will, steal some horses, and just go." He struggled to keep his voice low. They stood under the shelter of the blacksmith's shop. The smell of charcoal soaked into their clothing, and the banked forge warmed their backs.

Daniel's mouth rounded in shock. "I'm no horse thief. They'd hang us both if they caught us, and I can't rescue you again if my neck is in a noose beside you."

Jim's throat constricted, and his breath snagged, making it hard to swallow. He blinked the sensation away.

"Besides," Daniel said. "I can't choose for another man. I can't make Will return with us of his own accord, and I'm not about to force him. He'd just come straight back here. And I can't go back to my wife empty-handed. The best we can do is stick by his side and protect him."

Jim shook his head. He ran a hand over his face and through his hair. "Death is coming. I can feel it. And not a glorious one."

Daniel put a hand on his shoulder. "The rest of the men think we'll be staying here and not retreating. There's no safer place in Tejas y Coahuila right now."

Impotence shut Jim's mouth. In that moment, holding flimsy scraps of the future in his hands, he understood what Eva and Pump must feel like all the time.

Chapter 7

Eva

Sanctum, Axis Mundi, the True line

Homesickness pulled on Eva's heart, making it harder to concentrate. Instead of listening to the theology lesson, she stared past the handsome, dark-haired boy on her left and out the classroom window. It had been two weeks since her recruiter had brought her to Axis Mundi and the sanctum, and the novelty had worn off. Shame battled with her silly feelings, reminding her that home wasn't real. It never had been. Hadn't her recruiter spent the last year proving this to her? The love she'd received from her family had been a phantom, a program set to run on autopilot. When she cried for her mother at night, she felt like a fool.

The dark-haired boy noticed her daydreaming and followed her gaze. He'd sat beside her the day before, and her heart skipped a beat to find him next to her again. Together, they watched tiny members of Lux Libera cross the grounds below on important business. Master Singh scrawled looping cursive scriptures and their appropriate interpretations on the chalkboard, and the scratching grated on her ears.

"This so boring," Sakura said, voice lowered to fly beneath their teacher's droning monotone. "Why this first class in novitiate? When we do combat skills?"

The dark-haired boy smiled in Eva's direction before she turned her head to her roommate, Sakura. When Eva had first arrived, they had been randomly assigned to share bunks, but she could barely understand the girl's thick Japanese accent. Despite their communication issues, she admired her new friend. Sakura could already speak some English, whereas Eva knew none of her new roommate's native language.

"I don't know. I hate —."

"Eva!" Master Singh threw a nub of chalk and nailed her on the forehead. "Stand up."

Eva's ears burned and her vision tunneled as she shoved back her chair.

"When do we *not* speak in class?"

"When you are speaking, sir."

"Why do we not speak in class?"

"Silence is essential to deepening my relationship with God."

"And what is the punishment for breaking the holy silence?"

Her hands started to shake. "Cani—."

The dark-haired boy's chair screeched against the hard floor as he shot to his feet. "Monsieur Singh, s'il vous plaît. I broke the silence. Not Eva."

The teacher put a hand on his hip, and Eva jerked her head in the boy's direction, confused.

"Monsieur, she was telling me to be quiet. I was asking her a question about the Admonishments, but I should have waited until you allowed discussion."

Master Singh narrowed his eyes and cocked his chin. "Then perhaps *you* would like to answer my question?"

"Caning, sir."

"Yes, caning. Come forward, boy."

Eva's fear and embarrassment rooted her in place, and she watched the shifting narrative as if she were merely a bystander. The boy threaded his way through the desks and stood before their instructor, head bowed.

"Remove your shirt."

While Master Singh retrieved his bamboo staff from the corner, the boy complied. Circular scars dotted his bare shoulders and arms.

"Face your classmates."

The boy rotated on the ball of his foot and gazed above their heads at the back of the small room. With the first stroke, his eyes watered. On the third and final stroke, he grimaced but never cried out.

"Dress, please, and face me."

When he turned, Eva saw blood pricked in stripes across his back before he gingerly let his shirt down.

"What do you say?"

"Thank you for your discipline, Master Singh."

"Where are your hands and eyes? Try again."

The boy corrected his posture, placed a hand on his breast, and inclined his head. "Thank you for your discipline, Master Singh."

"Good. Now take your seat. Remember to include this in your weekly confessional. If you break the silence again, you will receive five strokes during general assembly."

Eva's mouth hung open as she watched the boy return to sit next to her. Except for his red face, she would never have known he had just been caned. He winked at her before he sat down and leaned forward over his desk to avoid the back of his chair.

As they left the classroom, Eva told Sakura she would meet her in their dormitory later and followed the boy down the spiral staircase. When they reached the bottom, she fell into step beside him. He glanced at her.

"I'm Eva."

"I know," he said, winking again. "I'm Tophe."

"You didn't have to do that."

"They make girls take off their shirts for canings, not just the boys. In my birth line, a girl would be embarrassed by such a thing. Maybe yours, too, no?"

Eva rounded her eyes in horror at the prospect of stripping to her bra in front of the class. Or would they make her take her bra off, too? Her gratitude doubled, filling her heart to bursting. "Thank you. I would have been super embarrassed," she said, grasping his hand. "It looked like it hurt. A lot."

He stopped walking and shrugged. "It's nothing I haven't felt before. Just don't talk again, yes? I don't want a caning during general assembly." Fear kept his smile from reaching his eyes.

"I won't talk. I promise."

His grin brightened.

"May I look at your back? There's blood on your shirt."

Tophe nodded, and they ducked into a sheltered breezeway. When Eva raised the cloth from his torso, he hissed. None of the cuts were deep, but she blew on them like her mother would have to take the sting away.

"Do you get in trouble a lot?"

"No, never. I don't break the rules here."

"Then how —?"

"My stepfather liked to… how do you say… tenderize me, like meat."

Eva lowered his shirt, and he turned around.

"What are the circles on your shoulders and arms?"

"He also liked to use me as an ashtray. Said he was toughening me up. Making me a man. The happiest day of my life was when I found out my birth family wasn't real."

"Even your mom?"

Tophe lifted a shoulder and dropped his eyes. "She did little to stop him."

"I miss mine. My mom and dad. My brother and sisters. My family was good to me. Sometimes, it's hard to believe they weren't real. They felt real. Like really real." Eva imagined her mother's arms around her and nearly cried in front of him.

"Mine never felt real. I always knew I belonged somewhere else."

"Even here, where you might be caned?" Eva asked.

Tophe considered her question with puckered lips. "I never knew when my stepfather would hit me. It didn't matter what I did or didn't do. Here, the rules are clear. If I don't break them, I'll be okay." He bobbed his chin at her. "You should be more careful. Novitiates who break the rules disappear. A boy on my floor was there one day and gone the next, but he was always getting into trouble. Older boys warned him, but he didn't listen."

"Where do they go?"

"My friend Enrique thinks they send them to the Abyss."

Eva put a hand over her mouth.

"Don't worry, though," he said. "Follow the rules like me, and you'll be okay. We're lucky to be here. Imagine the kids like us who Lux Libera hasn't found yet. They're living a big lie, no? At least we know the truth."

"I'm glad to know what's real, I guess."

"Yes, see?" Tophe said, lifting a hand. "It's for the best."

Eva didn't want their conversation to end. He was the first person in Axis Mundi who seemed to care about her. "What do you have to do this afternoon? Do you like cards? I could teach you my favorite game."

"I'm pretty good at cards. You'll have a hard time beating me, no matter the game."

Eva smirked. "We'll see about that."

El Copano

That evening, alone in their tent, Eva chewed on her thumbnail.

Tophe undressed, pulling the suspenders off his shoulders. "We'll be back on track tomorrow," he said. When she didn't answer, he bent down to put his face in front of hers. "Did you hear me?"

"What? Yes. Back on track." She crossed her eyes, trying to focus on him.

"Want to play a round of Egyptian Rat Screw?" he asked. It was a game she had taught him the day they had met as children. He stuck his leg out to her.

She turned her back to him and tugged on the heel of his boot. "Sure."

He gave her his other foot, and she pitched both boots into the corner.

"Hey, you'll mess up the polish. I worked hard on that," he said.

Eva dug in the knapsack he carried for both of them.

"You know, I was thinking," Tophe said. "We should carry duplicate supplies… in case we're ever separated again."

"Mmmm," she responded as she rummaged for her knives and pistol, then tossed them on her cot. She found the cards and fanned them out, enjoying the reminder of home. If timeline appropriate, they usually brought a deck along on missions. She snapped the fan closed, then eyeballed the deck, cutting it into equal stacks. She offered him first choice.

After she sat, they faced each other on Tophe's cot. He gestured to the space in front of him. "Loser first."

"I believe that would be you," she said, peering at him from under her brows.

Tophe knuckled his chin. "I believe that would be *you*, but your memory must be hazy. Head injury, right?" He waved an imaginary handkerchief. "I'll be chivalrous, though."

Eva pressed her lips together and cast her eyes to the heavens. "How kind of you."

Slowly, he laid his first card down, and Eva slammed hers on top.

The next moment, their hands flew. The deck she held grew and shrank as Eva won and lost cards. When she slapped a double, her jagged fingernail caught the side of his palm and drew blood. "Sorry," she mumbled.

He barely noticed, and his obliviousness jolted her conscience. There would never be a good time to explain all that had changed for her. She covered the untidy pile on the cot with both hands and looked up at him. "I need to tell you something."

With his next card poised to drop, he raised his brows.

"I lied to you yesterday."

His forehead wrinkled, and he dropped his hands, unconsciously squaring up his deck. "What about?"

"Pump."

His eyes widened. "I knew it! I knew there was something you weren't telling me."

Ashamed, she hung her head. "I'm sorry." She still didn't know how to start, but finally said, "Pump is a traveler like us."

His hands stopped moving. "What?"

"I know."

"That's not possible."

"It is. He showed me." She explained Pump's abbreviated novitiate. "He never took the final vows."

Tophe stared at the tent wall. "I didn't think anyone ever didn't take the final vows. I figured they threw people like that into the Abyss."

"Apparently not."

"Well, he's not marked like an excommunicant," Tophe said.

"No. He says he escaped."

"I get the feeling he doesn't like me."

In reluctant acknowledgment, Eva tilted her head to the side.

"Do you know why?" he asked.

"He doesn't like that I'm playing your wife."

"And why is that?" He held out his hand to her, and she put her half-deck in his palm. He added it to the stack on the bed, his eyes never leaving her face. Unable to meet his gaze, Eva watched his fingers close around the cards, tidying.

"Because the man who found me… I'm his wife now. I married him."

His hands froze.

She lifted her eyes.

"I'm sorry," he said. "I think I misheard you."

She didn't repeat herself.

They stared at each other.

"Please tell me I misheard you," he said.

Eva shook her head as fear closed a hand around her vocal cords. She shouldn't have told him yet. She wanted to pluck each word out of his ears and stuff them back down her throat.

"Eva," he whispered, horrified. His eyes searched hers. "No…" Fear to match her own drained his face of color. He cupped her shoulders and reverted to French. "You remember this is a shadow world, right? Nothing here is real. The people aren't real." He gazed over her shoulder and then back at her face. "No one ever needs to know. We complete our mission and go home."

When she realized he was blaming it on her head injury, she held up her hands. "I've forgotten nothing of Lux Libera's teachings. I… I just… don't… believe them anymore."

He lowered his arms, and a gulf opened between them.

"What do you mean, you don't believe them anymore?" His voice fell a dangerous octave, and his eyes hardened.

She wanted to shrink and darted her eyes to her out-of-reach knives. Of their own accord, her hands pushed at the bed, adding an inch of space. "I mean, I'm not sure anymore. I'm trying, but it's hard to believe this world is just a shadow when you've been here as long as I have." Guilt-ridden and terrified, she sucked her lower lip.

Tophe softened and grabbed her hands. "Listen, I think it's got to be normal to get confused after something like this happens. We'll get back to the sanctum, and you'll see."

"Yes," she said, squeezing his hands to hide her shaking. "I'm sure you're right." After a moment, she swallowed and peeked back up at him.

His head was turned toward Pump's tent, fierce eyes calculating. "I want to see what your *friend* can do tomorrow."

After Tophe had fallen asleep, Eva jumped inside Pump's tent, startling him. He sat in his undergarments, smoking a pipe, and turned bright red at the sight of her.

"I'm sorry," Eva said. "I just wanted to let you know I told Tophe, and he wants to see what you can do before he has to report for duty in the morning."

Pump inhaled and blew all the smoke out at once. "Have you told him everything?" he asked, looking meaningfully at her belly.

She shielded it with her hand. "Not yet." At the shake of his head, she said, "I told him what he could handle."

He stared at her out of the side of his eye and took another puff.

"Remember why we're here, Pump. This is about Francisca. Not me, Jim, or even Tophe. Convincing Tophe is just the key to keeping her safe."

"He's more than that, and you know it."

She glared at him and opened a portal to return to her tent.

"I'll be ready," he said before she stepped through.

Chapter 8

Eva

As Tophe and Eva dressed in the pre-dawn light, Pump materialized in their tent.

Gut instinct drew Tophe's pistol before he registered what was happening, and Eva stepped in front of her partner. She was torn between laughing at the shock on his face or yelling at Pump.

"Turnabout's fair play, huh, Pump?" she whispered in English, remembering how she had startled him the night before.

He shrugged, defiance in the set of his jaw. No laughter played in his dark eyes as he examined their sleeping arrangement of separate cots.

Eva pulled him down by the collar to place her mouth to his ear. "Yes, separate. You need to let that go. Nothing I'm doing here is betraying Jim." She pushed him away.

Pump straightened his shirt.

"How did you do that?" Tophe asked. He kept the pistol trained on Pump's chest.

Eva huffed and removed the gun from his hand. When he let her do it without resistance, she took it as a good sign.

In clipped tones, Pump explained how he traveled by looping the energetic strings in particles of air.

"That's heresy," Tophe said. "It's forbidden." He grabbed the pistol back from Eva and thumbed the hammer.

"What do you mean, it's forbidden?" Eva asked. "I'd never even heard of it."

Tophe glanced at her briefly and then firmed his grip.

"Why would the Elders declare something so useful to be heresy?"

Tophe lifted a shoulder. His eyes never left Pump's.

Confusion set in when she read uncertainty and guilt on her partner's face. "Did you know it was possible to travel other ways?" she asked.

As Eva watched him wrestle with himself, his jaw clenched. "Enrique discovered it. I asked the council about it." The hand holding the gun shook, then he dropped his arm and focused on Eva. "I thought we might use it in the field."

For a moment, her lungs refused to breathe. "You betrayed Sakura and Enrique." The words seeped from her lips, nearly soundless.

His features crumpled. "No… No."

White-hot rage flooded her face, burning her ears and cheeks.

As Tophe took in her reaction, he stuttered. "It wasn't like that. I mean, not intentionally. But yes, the council found out about them from me and investigated further."

"Why didn't you tell me?" She collapsed on her cot, her dress still unbuttoned, and put her head in her hands.

"How could I?" Tophe asked, his voice cracking.

When she raised her eyes, she saw tears welling in his.

The next second, he pulled out a handkerchief but only wadded it in his hands. "It doesn't change the fact they were fornicating."

With thoughts of the baby she carried, she sensed Pump watching her. She tilted her bowed head to the side and met his gaze.

Suddenly, the morning bugle call rang across the camp. Tophe blew his nose, splashed water on his face, and threw on the rest of his uniform. He studied Pump as he buttoned up his coat.

The older man stared back, unflinching.

At his revelation, Eva's scarred heart bled freely. She opened her mouth to tell him to stay but knew he had to go.

He kissed her on the forehead. "We'll figure this out." Without meeting her eyes, he snatched up his hat, ignored Pump, and left.

"Now, do you trust me?" she asked when he was gone.

Pump sat down on Tophe's bed, facing her. "I don't know what's gotten into me." He arched his fingertips, expanding and contracting the shape they formed. "I think he reminds me too much of my time with Lux Libera — what I could have become. All I feel is anger when I'm near him."

"I'm not sure if you've made our job harder or easier." Fresh tears spilled over her lashes when she thought of Sakura. "I can't believe…." She shook the rest of the words out of her head and wiped her eyes. "I don't think Jim would have been as jealous as you've been on his behalf." The very idea tempted her to wring his neck.

Pump snorted and cocked his chin.

"Regardless," Eva said, "the question of my fidelity — can we put it to rest?"

With a pat of the blanket, Pump surrendered. "Yes. I'm sorry."

"I need you to talk to Tophe calmly. Like you did with me."

Presidio La Bahía Goliad

Before dawn, word came from command to fire the artillery against their own walls.

"Guess we're actually leaving," Noah said. They shoved their fingers into their ears at the first boom.

"Stupid," Will said. "Fucking stupid."

Jim left the grumbling men and hid in the lumber. Though he tried, he couldn't sleep through the concussions. When the sun rose an hour later, fog and a gray sky obscured it, and Jim couldn't see from one end of the three-and-a-half-acre parade ground to the other.

Nearby, the forgotten oxen pawed the dirt, their protests becoming more insistent. Jim set a water bucket in front of his still-hitched horse. The animal had already drunk two other bucketfuls, and there was no feed to be found. As he stroked its neck, he recalled he had been willing to ride this pony to death, but it had performed with great heart despite being so thin from winter. He should steal it right now and charge out of the fortress.

Noah shouted and motioned for him to follow. With a nod of acknowledgment, Jim gave his four-legged temptation a firm pat and strode toward the chapel.

"Help us move the provisions," Noah said. "We're going to burn what we can't carry."

"The food?" Jim asked. "We're burning the *food*?" He glanced back at the overloaded buckboards, then flipped through his memories of passing crates down the brigade line. He didn't recall any rations being packed.

"Fannin's orders," Noah said. "Victoria's only about thirty miles from here. I guess Houston'll have provisions for us there. Leaves more room for ammunition. The Quartermaster is holding some back for breakfast before we leave."

Spohn, the dark-eyed Creole, placed his hands on his hips. "Is it also Fannin's orders to haul everything into the chapel? That seems assheaded and pointless, even for the Colonel. Why can't we just burn it in the yard?"

Noah threw up his hands. "Beats me," he said, scanning the roof. "Maybe he thinks it'll hide the smoke in the fog if it has to go through the windows? Keep the Mexicans from knowing we're abandoning the fort?"

Spohn arched his back and groaned to the sky. "As if blasting the walls with cannons doesn't give us away or anything."

Without another word, Jim carted rations to the rear of the chapel. At the same time, he filled his belly and stuffed his waistband with dried meat. The other men smirked at first but then copied him. The enormous pile, seven hundred head of cattle worth and all the cornmeal in the fort, billowed pooling black smoke beneath the vaulted stone ceiling. The waste nauseated Jim. Assured the blaze would grow, the men backed away and stepped outside where the smoke trickled, then poured, through the transom window above the chapel entrance.

As Jim walked past the blacksmith's, he saw the craftsman sink a glowing rod of iron into the touchhole of one of the largest cannons and break it off with a tap of his hammer. He crossed the parade ground, searching for Daniel. No sense of urgency drove the soldiers he passed, and he examined the sky with concern. Fog never lasted beyond the morning. Fannin couldn't have ordered better conditions for sneaking away. They should be on the road.

When he found Daniel, Jim handed him two-thirds of the meat he had hidden. "Share with Will. There's no more food until we get to Victoria, and there may not be food there. Fill your water pouches."

Worry shadowed Daniel's face. "I'm beginning to think we should have left last night like you wanted."

Jim gritted his teeth and peered around the fort. "There's nothing keeping us. Let's go."

"Will," Daniel said. "Will is keeping us."

Rather than lose his temper, Jim stalked away to wander the parade ground. Men unhitched baggage carts, freeing teams for hauling artillery. He counted nine cannons, leaving two buckboards for ammunition and several for baggage. When he remembered his own property, he ran to retrieve it. The axles of the wagon sagged under the existing weight, and Jim hesitated to add his items to the mound. He set them down as if laying a baby bird in a nest and stepped back when the axle squeaked.

With nothing left to do, he joined Spohn, Will, and Noah as they cooked breakfast and lounged to eat it. Jim consumed all he could, even to the point of discomfort, and measured the thinning fog against the climbing sun. Anxious to clear the walls, he paced.

After the men and gear were finally assembled, the officers gave the order to march. The few garrison women rode in the carts, and all filed through the southern wall's sally port. Over rough, virgin prairie, the vanguard led them down the river, hunting for an unguarded ford.

In the middle of the column, Jim marched with the rest of the Greys. As they exited the fort, the cannon in front of them veered off at a sharp angle, and the drover cursed, whipping the team. The oxen lowered their heads to the green, wet grass of the prairie and refused to move another foot. With more shouting behind them, Jim turned to see a team stepping backward at each command the drover gave, the wagon jackknifing.

"The Mexicans train their oxen differently," Spohn said, following Jim's eyes. "The volunteers don't know what the correct commands are." Another drover ran to consult with the hapless wagoner.

"Doesn't help that they were neglected all day and night, either," Jim said.

Spohn heard the accusation in his voice. "No, that doesn't help." He faced forward. "Not my responsibility."

As they marched, Daniel and Jim flanked Will in the line. The grind of wheels and the tramp of hooves and feet drowned out all other sounds, but Jim watched for signs of the enemy. Their slow, agonizing progress frustrated him. He could walk circles around the carts and not impede their way.

When they reached the river, the oxen stalled on the steep banks. Wheels slid under the weight of the heavy cannon while the Red Rovers aided the artillerymen in pushing from behind. They spent nearly an hour on the remaining guns, and Jim helped the men around him fish a howitzer out of the water.

In an effort to aid the animals, the wagoners offloaded some of their weight. Jim cried out when he saw his saddle tossed into the stream, along with a chest of musket provisions. Too heavy and awkward to carry twenty more miles on foot, he stamped down the urge to rescue it.

Cold and wet, they discarded more items along the way to pick up the pace. Even so, the oxen balked, and wagons broke down under the stress and had to be left behind. Jim marveled they had yet to be challenged, let alone sight the Mexican army.

Soon, a command to stop marching threaded its way through the ranks. The officers would let the oxen graze and the men rest, so they ground to a halt, spilling out onto the prairie.

The officers and heads of the volunteer militias moved away from the line to confer with Fannin. As Shackelford, leader of the Red Rovers from Alabama, yelled and gestured, red-faced and wild, in the direction they were traveling, Colonel Fannin stood with his arms crossed.

On the far horizon, a line of water-hungry trees indicated the safer shelter of a creek. The fog had burned away, and here on the prairie, they were completely exposed.

An arrogant smile danced on the lips of the other officers, and Fannin laughed at Shackleford. Westover and another officer agreed with the urgency of getting to Coleto Creek, but the majority overruled them. In frustration, Shackelford stomped back to his Red Rovers and fumed.

For once, the Greys agreed with Fannin.

"There's nothing to worry about," Will said. "We're the only militia here who's fought the Mexicans before. They're lazy cowards who can't shoot for shit. They probably won't even want to engage with us. We'll move faster once the animals are happy."

Over the boy's head, Jim and Daniel shared a look.

"I've never met a cowardly Tejano or Mexican," Daniel said. "I'd be careful underestimating them."

Will sniffed. "Whose side are you on?"

At the retort, the other Greys sneered.

Jim kept his mouth shut. Instead, he squatted alongside his shivering comrades and examined the growing hole in his left moccasin. Several men rolled cigarettes, offering one to Jim, but he politely declined. As the minutes ticked, Shackelford and Westover pressed Fannin to continue the march. He eventually relented, disgusted with officers so worried about their own skins.

At his command, the men regathered in formation. With the sun shining and his body moving again, Jim warmed up and dried out. Shouts ahead alerted them that another cart had broken down, and they all halted for the next hour while the supplies were sorted and spread amongst the remaining buckboards. As precautionary lookouts, four horsemen rode to the rear, the German boy Ehrenberg among them.

By mid-afternoon, the column advanced once again, crawling across the grass sea like a snail after a rainstorm. With less than two miles to go to get to the creek, vibrations rose through the soles of Jim's feet, and then he heard the volunteers behind him shout. A host of cavalrymen charged from the south, lances bristling. To the left and ahead, more converged on them in a coordinated advance. As the Mexican cavalry encircled the Texian army, a ripple of fear shot through his fellow Greys and washed over him.

Jim gripped his rifle to keep from racing to unhitch his own horse. He hadn't been on the wrong side since his family's wagon burned. The cavalry whooped and spun around them in a dizzying display of martial power, and the Greys responded with war cries of their own. Behind the whirling mass, the infantry arrived.

Chapter 9

Jim

The four horsemen of the rear guard swept past the Texian line in terror, kicking their spurs and thrashing their whips. Only Ehrenberg, the little German boy, yanked his horse to a stop and leapt down to join the army. To the shock of the men on the ground, the other three continued on past and rode unchallenged through the Mexican lines to rejoin Horton's Rangers, who had been acting as advance scouts and were now cut off. Jim added his voice to the Greys, cursing their cowardice.

"Were you fucking asleep, you goddamn bastards?" Spohn yelled. "How could you let them surprise us?" Red in the face, he spat the last words.

"No, this is good," Daniel shouted in his ear. "They can bring reinforcements from Victoria. I heard they have six hundred men there."

The other militias cheered at the prospect of battle. Their procession continued to creep forward, and Fannin rode near the center of the column. Without warning, the cavalrymen withdrew, making the way to the creek clear. Taking advantage of the hole, the Colonel ordered them to march at a normal pace, but Mexican infantrymen soon filled in the gap. The enemy surrounded them on all four sides but stood beyond the volunteers' rifle range. At the sound of a bugle, the Mexican formations lowered their muskets and pulled their triggers. Balls plopped harmlessly in the dirt outside the Texian lines.

The Greys howled with laughter. "Is that all you've got?" Ehrenberg called out in a thick German accent. "You must come closer if you want to kill us."

After a moment of indecision, Fannin raised his sword. "That's the signal for battle," he said. "I won't retreat another foot."

Jim's smile at Ehrenberg's taunt faded when he heard Colonel Fannin's foolhardy declaration. As one, the Greys turned the force of their hatred onto their own garrison commander. Pettus, their militia leader, ran to Fannin and pointed at the closer line of trees a mile away and on their left. "We have to change directions and get to Perdido Creek. Look at where we are, man!"

Fannin ignored him and shouted commands to close ranks and form a hollow square. Orders echoed up and down the line that stretched a quarter of a mile or more, and before and behind Jim, men and baggage collapsed to the center like an arching caterpillar. While the enemy kept pace on all sides, the Colonel skewed them toward the closer creek at a crawl.

With a loud crack, the remaining ammunition cart broke down, and Fannin called for them to halt and form their center around it. The Greys groaned at their position, a depression six or seven feet below the surrounding enemy.

"I'm not staying here," Spohn said, eyes wild. "We're not staying here."

Jim heartily agreed. As he primed his rifle, he scanned the enemy lines.

Spohn and the other Greys formed a wall behind their captain, Pettus, who continued to argue with Fannin. In a panic, two Greys unhitched a cannon and fired three ineffective shots at their enemy before Captain Westover shut them down.

"We go. Now," Jim said to Daniel. "There's a gap. Look. And there are three cart horses."

Daniel followed his finger and nodded, jaw jutting. He seized his brother-in-law's arm and pulled him around. Will's pale face stared back, frozen in shock. Even he now recognized no amount of bravado could save them from a disastrous fighting position.

Jim sent both men to gather a horse. As quickly as he could, he worked the buckles, clasps, and ties of his own. No one was paying any attention to him, but when he checked over his shoulder, he realized all the Greys were preparing to leave as well. His hands hovered, indecisive. It would be better to blend into the mutiny. When they charged between the formation and ran for the trees, the three of them could keep going. He caught Daniel's eye and jerked his head toward the cluster of men.

In answer, Daniel pointed behind Jim's shoulder and in the direction they were supposed to go. To his dismay, Mexican reinforcements were joining the existing soldados. The gaps all around them shrank. By Jim's count, they were now outnumbered three to one. The Greys' fierce anger devolved to rage. One man threw down his hat and cursed Fannin to his face. Westover shoved him back.

"We're here to stay, boys," Pettus, the Greys' leader, roared. "We're not going to let them buy our lives cheaply."

Without further argument, the Greys shifted into determined action. Along with the other militias, they stacked supplies into barricades and pushed carts into defensive positions. Some oxen broke free and ran toward the Mexicans. The soldados mocked the Texians as they opened a path in their ranks and swallowed the animals.

Jim helped position artillery at the corners, and one buckboard in the center was designated the hospital. There were enough smooth-bore muskets for each man to have three or four, and Jim took a moment to load each of his, including his own rifle. He primed two pistols and stuffed them into his belt.

The Texians formed three ranks of closely packed men around the interior of the square. By silent agreement, Jim and Daniel put Will behind them. Jim's shoulders rubbed against his neighbor's and Daniel's, while Will's rifle barrel would be next to his ear. No sooner had they positioned themselves than the enemy's bugles sounded, and the infantry and cavalry advanced on all sides.

"Hold your fire until I give the command," Fannin bellowed. Without hesitation, his orders were relayed down the square's perimeter. The difference in his voice startled Jim, but the Colonel stood straighter, eyes focused on the task ahead.

About a quarter of a mile away, the cavalry dismounted, and the infantry stopped to fix bayonets. Jim shifted his weight, and Daniel cast his eyes up and down their line. Jim ignored Will panting behind him. The Mexican officers raised their swords, and at the signal, the soldados positioned their muskets on their hips, firing again as one.

"Hold," Fannin repeated. His word reverberated as the shot pelted Jim's line. Sharp cries of surprise filled the air. Without penetrating, the balls struck heads and shoulders. Jim pulled at the neck of his shirt to examine the welting bruise rising on his chest. He rubbed the pain away and shared a nervous chuckle with the men beside him.

The enemy advanced again. The next volley flew over their heads, and Shackelford commanded his Rovers to kneel or sit. As if he were their own captain, the Greys obeyed the order and threw dirty glances at Fannin. Though the grass reached above their hats, shielding them from view, the illusion of cover gave cold comfort.

Jim peered down the barrel of his rifle, training it on the chest of the infantryman in front of him. He was within range. The man beside him fidgeted.

Daniel noticed Jim's finger moving to the trigger. "Don't," he said. "Wait. Put your rifle down."

Jim felt the eyes of the other men on him and lowered his weapon.

For a third time, the Mexican officers halted their foot soldiers. The crackling of their muskets rolled over the prairie in a syncopated wave, and a man, six feet from Jim, clutched his shoulder. Instantly, the line crimped around him as his fellows evaluated the wound. Several men cried out across the square. In the center, draft animals dropped to their knees and slumped to the side. An artilleryman fell.

Fannin's attention never wavered from the advancing line, despite the stock of his rifle being blown off. At one hundred yards, the enemy officers stopped their soldados. The remounted cavalry picked up speed, lances positioned for fatal thrusts, and the ground rumbled beneath the volunteers' knees. Flags snapped in the wind.

"Ready!" Fannin held his sword above his head.

Jim lifted his rifle to his shoulder with the Greys. He heard the Colonel's order to aim, but he was already trained on the same infantryman he had chosen.

"Fire!"

The cacophony of rifles, muskets, and cannons pounded like a hammer against his ears and chest. Smoke from the priming pans choked them, and Jim had no idea if he had hit his mark. When their view cleared, a roar rose from the Texians.

The point-blank range and artillery had devastated the advancing lines. Infantrymen ran sideways and collided with each other. Horses reared, threw riders, and trampled any unfortunates on the ground. An injured horse lay kicking in a pool of its own blood, its rider in pieces around it.

"Fire at will!" Fannin called.

Jim woke as if from a daze and grabbed from the pile of muskets at his knees. As quickly as they could be loaded, the artillery boomed.

The Mexican officers rallied their reluctant infantrymen at sword point, forcing them to charge the lines with bayonets.

Careless of his aim, Jim fired into the haze. When he ran out of muskets, he pulled his pistols from his belt. He tore at cartridge papers with his teeth and crouched between the hips of his neighbors to work the ramrod, reloading all his weapons at once, one after another. Each time he held his rifle, he aimed beyond the front line at one man farther back. For every enemy he nailed, grim satisfaction drew up the corners of his mouth.

The Mexican soldados' muskets were no match for the Texian's accurate rifles. It was suicide to come within the revolutionaries' longer range, and everyone knew it.

Dead and wounded artillerymen lay draped about the cannons. Pettus called for volunteers from the experienced Greys to man the guns.

As their lines thinned, Jim and Daniel spread themselves out. Will moved up between them. Jim darted his eyes at Daniel, questioning the boy's less protected position, but the other man looked away.

Since the first volleys, Jim's ears had cramped, and the sounds of war took on a muffled quality as if he were underwater. Several men around him left the line to advance through the smoke for a better shot. When Ehrenberg returned from one such adventure, he carried Mexican weapons and powder back with him. He claimed to have made it all the way to stand among the soldados without realizing it.

"Didn't you learn anything at Bexar, Ehrenberg?" Spohn shouted. "Don't use that Mexican powder. It clogs and misfires worse than ours! Don't you remember how I jammed my musket with ten balls before I realized I hadn't shot a single one?"

The boy growled in disgust and tossed it away.

As the afternoon dragged on, the artillery slowed. Will told Jim that the cannons needed to be cooled with water between each round, and the limited balls were dwindling. It went without saying they had no water to spare for bathing metal.

Jim left the line to retrieve more ammunition for the muskets. Having fired the last custom shot for his rifle, it lay useless to him now. The garrison supplies wouldn't have his smaller caliber.

As he passed Fannin, the Colonel pulled a bloody handkerchief from his trouser pocket, and a ball fell into his hand. Fresh red blood poured down his thigh, and one of his aides pressed a cloth to the hole. Though two other wounds wept, he still stood. Jim thought he might be a fool, but he wasn't a coward. He'd give him that, at least.

Jim jogged past the blanketed dead and the hospital cart overflowing with the severely wounded. One woman tended to a soldier, and a man lying nearby clutched at her skirts and begged for water. Her shoulders hunched over her ears as she ignored him, and a streak of blood ran across her nose and forehead. Even more red stained her dress and sleeves.

As he reached the ammunition wagon, three Mexican scouts cowered beneath it. They had been taken captive back at Goliad, and he had forgotten about them. Balls rained on the buckboard and flew through the spokes, causing them to jump. With their bare hands, they scraped at a hole in the thick turf of the prairie. Another volunteer approached the wagon and saw what Jim had seen. They shared a dark laugh and gathered what they needed.

When a ball nailed him in the kidney, Jim yelped. He lifted his shirt to inspect, but it was just another welt. A second pinged him in the head, and he ducked into a crouch. His eyes stung, filling with tears, and his hand came away bloody, but it didn't seem more serious than a cut. One of the Mexican prisoners cackled, pointing at Jim's face and rocking on his ankles. The other two evaluated him with flinty eyes. Jim didn't know if he should scowl back at the two or laugh with the one. He stared at their dark faces and thought of the Indios far to the south, where it was never cold, and a Nʉmʉ warrior could capture a long-tailed bird of every color. These men weren't in Tejas by choice. He decided to laugh with the hysterical man. In hindsight, he should have helped them escape. It was all so ridiculous.

After he ran back to his place in the line, he rejoined the fight. The cavalry had long since given up, and riderless horses, trapped between the lines, careened around the battlefield as a frightened herd. The cries of the wounded competed with the retorts of firearms and incessant bugle calls. Smoke drifted in heavy, noxious clouds to obscure their view. Around them, the lightning flashes from the pans, followed by the thunder of the guns, reminded Jim of an autumn storm throwing tornadoes as it advanced. The setting sun cast a sickly yellow hue over all.

With twilight, shots from the enemy side slowed and then ceased. As the smoke cleared, the Mexicans retreated from the growing breastwork of mangled bodies and dead horses. The ceasefire stretched long enough for more breathable air to return.

Jim peeked over his shoulders and saw the other enemy lines had fallen back. An eerie silence reigned. Trying to dislodge the uncomfortable pressure in his ears, Jim opened his jaw wide. He lifted his water pouch but found it empty. He didn't know when he had drunk last, and thickened saliva coated his mouth like resin.

Daniel tapped him on the shoulder. Black powder covered his teeth and right cheek to the ear. He held up his water, offering him a sip. Jim waved his hand, and Daniel passed it to Will. The boy took a short drink and handed the thin pouch back. Just then, a rifle cracked, and Will bent in half with a cry.

Chapter 10

Eva

El Copano

Pump preferred not to eat with the officers that night, though he agreed to help her talk to Tophe afterward. When Eva met up with her partner at the dining tent, his worried eyes belied his confident manner. The shadow lifted as she squeezed his hand. When she asked him how his day had been, Tophe scrunched his shoulders. "I've had my fill of being a paper-pushing Mexican cavalry lieutenant," he said into her ear. "Much nicer when we didn't arrive too early." He flexed his wrist and stretched his ink-stained fingers.

On cue, Francisca and her husband, Captain Telesforo Alavez, arrived. He served as Paymaster for the Cuautla Cavalry Regiment. Introductions were made, and Eva approached Francisca like a long-lost sister. "It's so nice to have another woman close to my own age," she said, taking her hands.

Francisca glowed, just as she always did. With her quick wit, dark hair, and flashing black eyes, she commanded an effortless presence and beauty Eva envied, and Eva wondered how she could have ever thought the Angel was simply a shadow. Between herself and her partner, they had snuffed Francisca's spark so many times she feared for the woman.

They took their places at the table, and the conversation proceeded as if scripted. Eva shared a tiny, knowing grin with Tophe and pulled out her handkerchief in anticipation. The next moment, Captain Alavez sneezed on his neighbor, unable to cover his mouth in time. His ears turned red, and Eva offered the cotton square to him under the table. Across from her, Francisca sat next to Tophe.

"I heard you recently arrived from San Patricio," Eva recited. "What news?"

"Yes," Captain Alavez said after swallowing his bite. "We took the town easily from the rebels. Half their force was out stealing horses from law-abiding ranches, and we were able to kill or capture all of them. The gringos still in camp were caught off-guard." His fork hovered above his plate as he addressed the ladies. "General Urrea offered them their lives if they would lay down their arms. We were fighting house to house, and those Norteamericano settlers and native Tejanos still loyal to Mexico were getting hurt." He scooped up another bite. "They refused, despite being outnumbered. We, of course, overwhelmed them and captured the entire unit… well, those that weren't killed outright."

"And what happened to the prisoners, Captain Alavez?" Madam Jimenez, one of the officer's wives, asked.

Before he could answer, Francisca piped up. "Father Molloy and I interceded with the General on their behalf."

Captain Alavez frowned at his wife, his face flushing, and gripped his fork.

Father Molloy inclined his head. "Yes, it was a close thing, too. They already had the prisoners lined up to be shot. We convinced the General to march them off to the prison in Matamoros instead."

"Well," Madam Jimenez said, "I certainly wouldn't have shown mercy to such unfeeling, impious creatures. I, for one, support the President's decree. It's important to be firm; otherwise, we may find every state in open revolt."

Though Eva had heard her say those words during other missions, she saw the older woman with new eyes. Before her was a real person, and she no longer felt like she was watching a movie play out in front of her, where Madam Jimenez's views had no consequences. The men smiled at the older woman, but when she glanced at her plate, they traded sly smirks with one another.

"I'm not terribly concerned about our other states," her husband, Captain Jimenez, said. "It's just Tejas that is proving to be unruly. After Zacatecas, the fires of revolution have burned less brightly."

"Repression works," Captain Alavez said. "It's dangerous to show mercy." He looked everywhere but at Francisca.

When the meal concluded, the men stood together to discuss a logistical matter, and the women gathered to the side. Captain Alavez peeled himself away and strode over to collect Francisca. He clasped her arm above the elbow, and she hid a wince. Francisca bid them all goodnight, and off-script, Eva reached out to grasp her free hand.

"Let's visit tomorrow," she said. Tophe's brow furrowed as he darted his eyes at her.

Francisca smiled. "I would like that. Until then."

Captain Alavez bowed in the women's general direction and led Francisca out of the tent.

"She's not his real wife, you know," Madam Jimenez said. "He abandoned his legitimate wife, Maria Augustina, and two small children in Toluca. Maria is a distant relative of mine."

The other women gasped and shook their heads. When they turned to Eva, she knew she was supposed to fall in line as she always did, but Eva couldn't. She didn't know the circumstances that separated Maria from Telesforo or brought him and Francisca together. Maria was probably safer away from him. Instead, Eva said, "I know."

Confused brows creased around her. Madam Jimenez tightened her shawl against the chill and shifted her shoulders. Tophe appeared at her side, and as if nothing were amiss, the women beamed at his good looks.

Once free of the officers' dining tent, he said, "Let's go for a walk."

Mist coated her cheeks, and Eva squinted up at the sky. "Are you sure?"

He shrugged. "It's barely anything. You're not going to melt."

She took his arm when he proffered it. As they walked by the cookfires of the camp, the enlisted soldiers sang and laughed, and camp followers sat hip-to-hip next to their men or in laps.

Beyond the glow of torches, Tophe led her toward the shore path and a rocky outcropping. They passed lovers in the grass and kept walking. Waves crashed against the empty wharf. The crumbling cliff of the coastline wouldn't turn into sand for another half a mile.

Tophe halted and scanned the area, then switched to French. "We'll have to take care of your friend before we leave."

Eva swallowed. She opened her mouth, but he continued, "And how much does the other man… the one who took care of you? How much does he know?"

"He doesn't know anything," she said, shouting above the surf to be heard. Darkness shrouded his face. She had never lied to Tophe like this. She hardly recognized herself, glad he couldn't see her eyes.

"Have you…" He didn't finish his question. "Never mind. Don't answer. I don't want to know."

Her hand crept over her stomach. "I'd like you to talk to Pump. He's been to many more worlds than we have. He's seen things we didn't know existed."

Like a slab of obsidian, her words threw up a wall between them, and Tophe froze, silent on the other side.

She reached her hand toward his but didn't touch it. "There are other groups like Lux Libera. We're not the only ones who can travel."

"Heretics, Eva," he said, his voice steely. "They must all be heretics. Only Lux Libera is the true way. You know what the scriptures say."

"Yes, and I can quote them as well as you can." Her voice rose in pitch. "This isn't a shadow world, Tophe. These people are real. What we're doing is wrong."

"Enough! That man has infected you with lies." He grabbed the tops of her arms and shook her once, making her bite her tongue. "You have to forget these things. You know what will happen to you!"

"The council never has to know," she said, tasting iron.

"I agree. We complete our mission, go home, and never speak of this again."

Eva weighed her words. "I want to leave Pump alone. There's no need to kill him."

"It's better than torture and the Abyss. If he's truly your friend, you'd want to help him be reborn."

"Lux Libera has left him alone this long. Unless we told them, there's no reason to think they will go after him now."

"What is time to Lux Libera, Eva?" He released her and took a step back. "Besides, we can't *not* tell the council about him. We either take care of him ourselves, or we tell the Elders."

The paradox snarled into a hopeless tangle in her brain. How could she be here and now with Pump, and at the same time, out of time, Lux Libera could kill him at an earlier point? Such acts must spin off, creating separate timelines. It was the only way that she could comprehend it. This version of Pump, the version she loved, should be safe, but she didn't know for sure. If they could kill Francisca, someone else could kill this Pump.

Tophe paced in front of her.

"Please. I'd rather we leave Pump alone, *and* we don't tell. I can't kill him."

He dismissed her concern with a silhouetted wave. "Don't worry. I wouldn't make you do it."

She yanked his wrist and pulled him to a stop. "No, I don't want you to kill him, either. Let his choices play out for themselves."

His featureless head shook. "I think it's cruel, Eva," he said. "You're not a cruel person." When she didn't answer, he paced again. "I don't make any promises. I don't like what he's done to you. That alone is worth death. Who else has he turned against righteousness?"

"Maybe I can convince him to join Lux Libera," Eva said. "He was nearly there. I think Pump might be open to it, especially as this line is about to merge with the True line. He thinks the people are real and distinct. He will see how wrong he is after we kill Francisca, and this line no longer exists as a separate entity. He'll see, for instance, his wife here combines with his wife in Axis Mundi since they are both Fated." She hesitated, trying to wedge herself back into her old beliefs without falling into a philosophical hole. "And there will be a Fated doppelgänger of himself in the True line. He'll be the only person he knows who won't merge. It will prove his beliefs are wrong."

A sudden thought hit her. If they had indeed been merging lines, how had they not gotten stuck in Axis Mundi's past or somehow been obliterated or thrown out into the Abyss? It seemed so obvious to her now.

Tophe stopped pacing. He stood with his hands on his hips, his weight shifted to one leg.

Eva shivered, the mist soaking through her coat.

"Compromise?" he asked. "We give you two days to convert Pump. After we make our target, if he isn't willing to return with us to Lux Libera, we kill him." He turned his face toward camp, and the fires illuminated his teeth.

"Okay," she heard herself say.

Though their walk back had been quiet, the hairs on the back of her neck stood up as they moved through the grass. At their tent, she left Tophe and headed to Pump's to work on his conversion.

When she called through the canvas, the older man pushed open the flap. He had acquired a tallow lamp somewhere, and she wrinkled her nose at the stench. With only officers receiving cots, Pump had gathered Spanish moss to make a dry mattress on the soggy ground. He gestured for her to sit on his blanket.

"Where's Christophe?" he asked, joining her.

"He's not coming," she said. "He won't be won over by talking to you. Tophe has no interest in philosophy or physics or questioning the theology of our people." She sighed. "He never has. I should have known better."

Pump's shoulders relaxed, and he puffed out his cheeks.

"I shouldn't have made you come," she said. "If I had known he already knew about other travelers, I would have realized it was hopeless." She leaned her elbows on her thighs, and a single tear disappeared into the fabric of her skirt.

Pump put his hand on her bowed head. When she looked up, he let his hand fall to her cheek. "I don't begrudge you my aid, darling, but I didn't exactly come through for you either."

Eva tilted her head and pressed his hand against her face, closing her eyes. "It wouldn't have mattered if you were the most skilled persuader. Tophe is too principled and loyal."

She pulled his hand down onto her lap. "I have two days to convert you to Lux Libera before he kills you."

The guttering lamp threw ghoulish shadows across his face. Black smoke crackled and coated the peaked roof. As Eva watched him think through the possibilities, his head bounced lightly, eyes inward. He refocused on her. "Are you going to let him return to Lux Libera and tell the council about me?"

Without looking at him, she ran her fingers over the thick weave of the woolen blanket. "I don't know, Pump." Her fingernail caught on the fibers. "He doesn't know your full name or where you live."

His face grew hard, and he jerked his hand back from her lap.

Nausea bloomed in her gut. "You know what you're asking of me," she said through clenched teeth, incensed enough to hold Pump's eye. "I know you do. You might as well ask me to cut out my own heart."

He didn't respond.

"I think you should return to your wife," Eva said. "I will protect Francisca as long as she is in Tejas, and when it is safe, I will make my way to your relatives in Louisiana."

He chewed the side of his cheek. "Do you want me to bring Jim to you?"

"No. The less Tophe knows of Jim, the better, and right now, he knows nothing."

Pump nodded in agreement. She seemed to have passed a test. He opened his arms, and she entered his embrace. "I trust you to do the right things to keep us safe," he said. "And be careful. I can't shake the feeling we're being watched. Something's not right."

"I will be. I don't think things will feel right again until we're all back home." A breath shuddered raggedly through her lungs as she wished for Jim, wondering if he was still on the road or had arrived at Pump's relatives in Louisiana. "One thing before we part," she said. "I need you to punch me in the face."

Chapter 11

Jim

Battle of Coleto

Daniel and Jim unfolded Will and searched for blood. A ball whistled by Jim's ear, and he reached across to pull Daniel down with him. "Sharpshooter!" he cried. Where was Eva when he needed her? It was the first thought he had allowed himself of her, and he shoved her away.

Daniel raised Will's shirt and found a neat hole in the side of his belly, just under the bottom rib. Will groaned as they rolled him over to examine his back, but they found no exit wound. Daniel removed his coat and tore his shirt sleeve, pressing it to Will's stomach.

Rifle shots continued in bursts for the next twenty minutes. Based on sound alone, Jim thought he counted four gunmen. Spohn fired blindly into the smoke. The snipers concealed themselves in the grass, and Jim scanned the field for signs of their positions.

"Captain Duval!" Spohn called. To Jim and Daniel, he said, "He's the best marksman in the company."

Jim glanced over his shoulder toward the Kentucky Mustangs militia, a group of men he'd had little interaction with. One of their number pushed his captain's arm and pointed to Spohn. At the summoning, the officer ran across the hollow in a forced stoop and slid down next to them.

"We got some snipers in the grass, Captain," Spohn said. "We can't dislodge them."

"They're Indians. We've got them on all sides," Duval said. "I haven't gotten a bead on ours."

Nearly one hundred yards from them, Jim saw grass move opposite the direction of the wind, and he confirmed his sighting several moments later when the top of a head breached the surface. He pointed. "There."

Duval followed his finger but didn't see.

Puffs of smoke rose, blending with the wet haze, and four more men fell in the Texian line.

Duval smiled. "I've got'm." He lifted his rifle to his shoulder and waited. The grass moved as the snipers reloaded. The barest crown of a head appeared through the thinning cover, and Duval pressed the trigger. A burst of red fountained, and Spohn yelled in triumph, thumping Duval on the back.

Over the last hour of dusk, Duval watched for the next opportunity. Men dropped in threes, and then twos, and finally, with long intervals between, in singletons. In the twilight, the remaining sniper's pan flashed, alerting them to his position.

Duval calculated the angles, then howled in pain at the same time his rifle cracked. Blood leaked through his knuckles as he cradled his hand to his chest. Jim forced him to open his fingers. A bloody stub dripped where the pinky of his right hand should have been. They hunkered down, waiting for another man to fall, but none did.

"I think you got him," Spohn said.

"Good," Duval replied. He squinted at his hand. "Filthy Inj—." His eyes darted to Jim and skittered away.

The other snipers surrounding the formation realized the danger darkness brought and retreated for the night. With the respite, Jim laid on his back and allowed himself to close his eyes. His tongue stuck to the roof of his mouth.

Daniel poked him. "Let's get Will to the hospital."

Each draping an arm over their shoulders, they helped the boy to stand. Will shrieked when he tried to walk, so Daniel and Jim formed a chair with their arms and carried him the rest of the way. Dozens of seriously wounded men lay around the wagon, including the Greys' Captain Pettus, but actual deaths seemed low. Jim counted ten blanket-covered bodies, mostly artillerymen. After finding an empty spot on the ground for the boy, Daniel gave Will his coat as a pillow. They had nothing else. A woman pressed more bloody fabric to his wound and called for one of the two doctors.

With Will settled, they drifted toward the growing cluster of men surrounding Colonel Fannin. A fine mist fell, and Jim crossed his arms over his chest. Fannin leaned on one of his aides, speaking to the group. "… the first of the two options is to make a run for the timber of Coleto Creek under cover of darkness; the second is to hope for reinforcements from Victoria that must arrive by morning."

The men grumbled, already divided.

"I believe after the whipping the enemy received today," the Colonel continued, his volume increasing to keep pace with the side arguments, "they are too busy licking their wounds to give us much of a challenge, but they will surely be reinforced overnight. If we are to make an escape, now is our chance."

At this, the Greys perked up.

"On the other hand, we cannot flee with our wounded. There are no surviving draft animals," Fannin said.

Spohn rolled his eyes and huffed.

Ehrenberg gazed around at his fellows. "I say we leave, and I think I can speak for all the Greys. This is our only hope. We've heard what happened to the men at the Alamo. We can't depend on the honor and humanity of our enemy."

Spohn raised his voice. "It's better for most of us to survive to fight another day rather than sacrifice our entire company."

A Kentucky Mustang answered back, "You're asking us to leave our wounded friends and relatives to be butchered. My family would never forgive me. I could never forgive myself."

"And you're asking us to sacrifice ourselves for them!" Spohn shouted. "To what end? How does that help the cause?"

Fannin stared at the ground. Over the bickering, the wails of the dying formed an eerie backdrop.

"Comrades, listen to the cries of pain from our brothers. Are we willing… are the Greys of New Orleans, the first company to enter the field for freedom, *willing* to leave their wounded to the horrible death Mexico has sworn to them?" Fannin clenched his fist and met the eye of each man circling him. "Before dawn, Horton should arrive with six hundred men. Ward is still on the run with one hundred of our brothers. If he has heard our cannon, he could even now be waiting in the woods to join our reinforcements."

The men murmured at the thought of a flanking force that could pinch Mexico in the middle.

"Friends, I beg you," Fannin said, "by the good in your hearts, do not abandon the helpless ones here. At least give them protection until the break of day. If no help is here by that time, I will follow you!"

Jim peeked sidelong at Daniel, who hunched beside him. "It makes no sense to stay until morning," he whispered.

"I agree," Daniel said. "Can we carry Will without being detected?"

"We have to try; otherwise, we're dead men." Jim studied the dark sky. "There will only be a sliver of moon tonight, even if the clouds part."

The Greys huddled together to discuss. Jim heard one man point out that Pettus was so wounded he would need a buckboard or a stretcher.

"Pettus would be the first to tell us to leave," Spohn said.

Ehrenberg jabbed his thumb over his shoulder. "None of the other militias are willing to abandon the wounded. We will be even more outnumbered if we leave on our own. We'd be unstoppable if we had everyone in the timber. But with just us...." He wagged his head.

His audience shifted their feet. A cry for water pierced the night, and the men grimaced.

"I think we must stay, boys," Noah said. "There are Greys among the wounded. We are superb fighters — our rifles against their muskets. You saw the hundreds of Mexican dead today. We may be able to win the day tomorrow."

None of the men responded. Jim thought of his own rifle lying useless on the ground.

After the silence dragged on for nearly a minute, Spohn was the first to storm off. "Let's get busy fortifying then," he said, spitting the words over his shoulder.

In a low voice to Jim, Daniel said, "We should wait an hour or so."

Jim nodded and then followed Spohn, who was back at their line digging a trench with his Bowie knife. Jim drew his own and scraped, piling dirt onto the inadequate breastwork. Daniel joined others who hauled dead draft animals, carts, and baggage outside the lines.

Mud covered Jim from head to toe. He tried to swallow, but his throat stuck to itself. He pushed his sleeve back and wiped away the dirt from his forearm with a grimy hand, then held it out to the mist. While he waited, he opened his mouth to the sky. The moisture did nothing to wet his mouth, much less quench his thirst. After a moment, he licked his arm but came away with nothing that helped.

"Did that work?" Spohn asked.

"No."

Jim returned to scraping and ignored the pounding in his head. The mist soaked to his skin, and an icy wind cut through his clothes. With no hope of building a fire, at least the digging kept him warm. He noticed his hair dripping and placed a lock in his mouth.

"Never thought I'd wish for long hair like a woman," Spohn said. His raspy laugh died away when he clutched his throat. After several beats, he asked, "Can there be worse rain? It's freezing us, ruining our last good guns, and we can't drink it."

Just as Jim was about to stand to find Daniel for their escape, three musket shots rang out in quick succession. Men ran to their positions and checked their powder. For about half an hour, nothing more happened. The campfires of the enemies glowed on the horizon, and faint singing floated toward them on the breeze.

"Wonder what they're eating," Noah said.

"I'm not even hungry anymore," Spohn said. "I just want a drink. Whiskey, water, beer. Don't care. It's all I can think about."

Heavy footsteps tramped behind them, and then Daniel materialized, taking up a musket on Jim's right. "The Mexicans caught and executed three of our men who were deserting," Daniel said. "At least… three men from the Red Rovers are missing.

They didn't want to stay. The officers think it must have been them."

Jim cursed under his breath.

"Cowards," Spohn said. "Guess we can relax then since the Mexicans aren't attacking us."

Jim's mouth gaped at his hypocrisy, but the man couldn't see his expression in the dark. After a moment, Jim nudged Daniel on the arm and said, "Let's check on Will."

When they reached the hospital area, the incessant chorus of weeping grated on their nerves. Those men crying and begging for just a swallow of water seemed to be out of their minds, and those caring for them couldn't convince them there was nothing to give.

Will moaned, unconscious, in imaginary conversation with his mother. While Jim felt his feverish forehead, Daniel tapped his face and called his name. His brother-in-law tried to lift him, but the boy cried out, so he lowered him back down, then slapped his cheeks.

Frustrated, Jim straightened and turned his back on Will and Daniel. He could make it through the Mexican lines on his own. He didn't know if Daniel could move quietly, but there was no question that Will couldn't control his noise.

After several more ineffective slaps, Daniel gave up. "You should escape without us."

Jim hesitated for only a moment. "No." He heard the word come out of his mouth. His head and heart were in conflict, but he knew the right answer. "In another world, I'm already dead. In this world, I owe you my life."

At first, Daniel didn't respond but then placed a hand on Jim's shoulder. "Thank you."

All night, they stayed in position as false bugle blasts kept them on edge. Like rats trying to sleep on the edge of a half-filled cup, every man jerked awake. Two of Jim's muskets and both pistols had clogged over the course of the afternoon, leaving him with only two firearms. He had no idea where his bow and quiver were.

Aware of each second that passed, the long intervals of silence and complete darkness allowed fear to creep in and sit on his shoulders. Jim strained his ears for the sounds of reinforcements arriving, but they never appeared. He imagined the Mexicans could hear the cries of their wounded. Black figures crept around the battlefield, collecting fallen and injured enemies. The Texians shivered in place, and Jim thought his teeth would crack.

All the defenders crouched in position along the perimeter of their formation or were incapacitated. In the small hours, Jim returned alone to the ammunition wagon. He bent down and peered underneath. "Todos ustedes van," he whispered. None of the Mexican prisoners moved. "Vamanos," he tried again. He cocked a thumb over his shoulder, placed a finger over his lips, and then removed it. This failed to earn a response either, but he doubted they could see more than his outline, so he stood up and walked away.

Back at his position, Spohn and Noah decided to dig a seep hole. Jim joined to stay warm. Out of sheer exhaustion, they gave up, their thirst more powerful than before they started. With that task abandoned, Jim paced the interior of the camp's fortifications to distract himself. When he checked later, the space under the ammunition wagon was empty.

Chapter 12

Jim

By first light, Jim's swollen tongue filled his throat, and he poked at the hard, dry spot in the middle. He had experienced such thirst during certain ceremonies and once on a forced march to safety with his people. To conserve their meager supply for the children, the adults had threatened each other with death if they tried to drink. No noble reason accompanied the suffering this time.

The men the Texians called Indians had not been able to collect all the Mexican dead overnight. Dozens still lay across the battlefield, alone and in groups. Jim and the other men glanced toward Victoria, searching for friendly riders, but it became a habit that no longer made sense.

Noah groaned and gestured at the soldados positioning a howitzer and two four-pounders on the hill. The slow-moving Mexican artillery had caught up with their army overnight. The Texians had stood a chance against an enemy with no big guns, but now the game changed in an instant. Jim imagined the barricades in front of him splintering under a well-placed blast. They sat naked on the prairie.

Beyond the safety of their hollow square, Ehrenberg wandered the battlefield. Jim and other men joined him to inspect the dead. After ignoring the first bodies, Spohn began checking pockets for valuables. One man startled awake at his touch.

"No… por favor… por favor, por favor." The man cringed away, raising his hands to ward off an attack. Spohn drew his knife.

"Hey! Hold on," Noah said. "Let's take him back and question him. You speak Spanish, right?"

"A bit."

"We'll come back for him," Ehrenberg said. "He's not going anywhere."

When they came across another soldado still alive, they agreed to retrieve him as well.

"Look!" Noah said, holding up a muddy enemy banner against the golden mist of dawn.

Spohn acknowledged it with a disheartened lift of his chin, and Noah lowered his arm, smile fading. Smoke from the Mexican campfires and the scent of their own roasting oxen drifted toward them. A tiny soldado on the hill saluted them with a mug in his hand. He took a long drink and poured out the remainder.

"Bastard," Spohn said.

Noah laughed and couldn't stop, then bent over double. Ehrenberg told him to shut up. When they returned to camp, Noah tossed the enemy banner against the clutter of a barricade.

As they entered, a woman and her young teenage son passed them on their way out, determined eyes set on the Mexican camp above them.

"Where are you going, Mrs. Cash?" Spohn asked. He gauged the other men's reactions to her behavior.

"To ask General Urrea for water," she croaked. "The wounded are dying without it. I can do nothing for them."

Spohn lifted a hand at her retreating back. "Shouldn't we stop her? Go with her?"

Noah shrugged.

"Maybe they'll take pity on a woman and boy and send us water," Ehrenberg said.

As the men hobbled under the weight of the prisoners, the Greys clustered around them, forming a parade. At their approach, Fannin grasped an aide's hand, who pulled him to stand.

After tedious questioning under Spohn's broken Spanish, they learned the remaining Mexican army numbered 1,900 men and expected more reinforcements that morning. Jim wasn't sure if Spohn's translation was correct. He searched for a better translator, but the last Mexican drover had run back to his people the moment chaos had set in.

The Greys widened their eyes at each other and grimaced. Between the artillery on the hill and the vast discrepancy in numbers, fighting their way to the timber seemed their only choice.

As if on cue, the well-rested and well-fed Mexican army stepped forward, ringing the lip of the bowl and surrounding them in an orchestrated show of force.

Every Texian face gazed up at the enemy. Flags snapped, breaking the silence, and a thin cry warned that the howitzer's fuse was being lit. More than one man ducked or ran to their positions as the ball sailed overhead.

Fannin tried to have a private conference with his officers, but the Greys crowded in, remembering past betrayals.

"We whipped them off yesterday, and we can do so again today," Fannin said.

The Greys competed with each other for his attention, arguing to fight their way through to the creek.

"We should have left last night," Spohn said.

"We could surrender if they will guarantee us honorable terms," a Kentucky Mustang said. "We make them promise to treat us like prisoners of war, not pirates or mercenaries. Get guarantees of parole."

Most Red Rovers sided with the Greys. They pointed over and over again to the slaughter of prisoners at the Alamo. Even some of the still-conscious wounded shouted over that they'd rather not lie there and wait to be murdered.

"Why would we think they will treat us any differently?" Spohn asked. "I am not surrendering. The *Greys* will not surrender. We will die fighting. With knives, if we have to!"

Another loud boom sounded from the hill, and the men stooped, looking over their shoulders. Again, Urrea had aimed beyond them.

The other militia spokesmen argued for surrender. Very few volunteers wanted to stay where they were and continue to fight, but neither did they think they could reach the woods. In the clear minority, the Greys and the Red Rovers doubled their efforts.

Fannin shielded his brow. He would open his mouth to speak but then close it again. Whenever a Grey spoke, he pondered the ground.

At the discussion of surrender, panic skewered Jim. Such a decision would be unthinkable if he fought alongside his brothers. But he reminded himself that Mexicans were not known for torturing or mutilating their prisoners, and there were no fleeing women and children at his back. He didn't need to remove his moccasins and fight to the death for a cause that wasn't his. With those thoughts, he locked eyes with Daniel's ashen face.

"I'm sorry," the man said.

When Daniel repeated himself, Jim clenched his jaw and waved his hand.

"We should be in position," one man observed. "They'll charge us at any moment."

Though many reclaimed their arms, reluctant Greys hung around Fannin and his officers. After returning to his position, Jim checked his muskets. He wagered they'd both be clogged after the next exchange.

At the third, lower, yet still harmless, assault from the cannon, all stared back at the Mexican army, readying themselves for the bugle blast sure to follow. Instead, the enemy raised a white flag, and a cheer rose from all but the Greys. Jim peeked over his shoulder. One of their own officers had flown a white flag. Jim wasn't sure if the Mexican flag had risen first or in answer to their own because Fannin had finally made a goddamn decision.

From the Mexican lines, a delegation of officers appeared and halted halfway across the battlefield while Fannin sent several of his officers to meet them. After the brief exchange, one of the Mexican officers returned to his camp. When he came back, one of the Texians brought a message to Fannin.

Ehrenberg was summoned to translate for the remainder of the negotiations. Mexican Colonel Juan José Holzinger was the only officer who spoke English, but too brokenly. Ehrenberg would translate the Texians' English into Holzingers' native German, and then Holzinger would translate into Spanish for his own side.

"Sure, I can translate for Johann Josef," he said, laughing. "Juan José. Who does he think he is? And how'd my fellow countryman get to be a colonel in the Mexican army?"

The morning dripped away as both armies watched the officers negotiate and run messages back and forth. Eventually, General Urrea insisted on speaking to Fannin directly. Shackelford stopped the Colonel before he crossed in front of Jim.

"If you can't get honorable terms, come back," the leader of the Red Rovers said. "Our graves are already dug. Let us be buried together."

Fannin placed a hand on his arm. "I will accept nothing less than surrender with honor." As he limped across the field supported by an aide, the Colonel paused to study one of the Mexican dead, then raised his head and continued.

Following the Colonel with his eyes, Jim rested his forehead against the barrel of his musket. Every defender focused on the negotiations, even the men on the other sides of the square. As time passed, Urrea's voice grew loud enough to be heard by the watchers, and after that, Fannin and his officers huddled to confer.

While they debated, Urrea set his hands on his hips and stared at the Texian army. Not one to miss an opportunity, Spohn made a rude gesture.

When Fannin finally spoke, a toothy grin broke across Urrea's face, and he clasped his hands together. The Greys grumbled at the sight of Urrea placing his arms around Fannin.

The moment Ehrenberg returned, they peppered him with questions.

"Fannin agreed to surrender all of our arms," he said.

Spohn rubbed his cheeks with both hands. "Fuck."

"But," Ehrenberg said, "we may keep our private property. We'll be shipped to El Copano or Matamoros and on to New Orleans and set free. We'll receive the same rations as the Mexican army while we're prisoners of war, and our wounded will be cared for."

As the Greys looked at each other, Jim's haunting fear dismounted from his shoulders.

"Our obligation," the German boy continued, "is our word of honor not to fight hereafter against the present government."

Spohn threw his musket down. "He's signed our death warrants! There's no way they'll keep their word."

Eyes wide, Noah and another Grey walked away.

One man gnashed his teeth and stomped on the ground. "There goes my land," he said, then pulled out a cigar, fury punctuating every motion.

Jim smiled to himself that none of these men would settle in Nʉmʉnʉʉ Sookobitʉ. Daniel grinned at him and left to check on Will.

When Fannin announced the terms of surrender, the other militias sighed, and anxiety cleared from their faces. But Noah and Spohn surrounded Fannin to harangue him with the other angry Greys. Jim stayed clear.

Across the lines, soldados wove their way through the battlefield to meet their former enemies eye to eye. Under armed guards, the men and boys accepting surrender piled their weapons in a stack secure from the formation. Jim gathered the muskets at his feet, including his, Daniel's, and Spohn's, and delivered them to the growing mound. With a double take in his direction, Spohn scowled. He stepped toward Jim as if to intervene, but then pivoted back to Fannin, raising his voice again.

Colonel Holzinger oversaw the surrender process with encouraging smiles. "In eight days, home and liberty, gentlemen."

The few capitulating Greys ignored him, but Jim nodded, encouraged when they labeled his weapons with his name. The man behind him opened his mouth and pointed at the three teeth remaining in his head, and the officer allowed him to keep his knife.

As the Mexicans entered the camp in high spirits, they sang a song Jim didn't recognize. One man approached Jim and pretended to shoot him with his finger. Jim threw up his hands and stuck out his tongue. The soldado laughed in surprise and continued on his way, but his companion glared as he strode past, drawing a line across his throat. Jim erased his expression and reached for his knife, but had forgotten he'd surrendered it.

When he felt a tap on his shoulder, a small man stood very close to him and held up a water pouch, eyes darting around them. Jim recognized him as one of the prisoners under the wagon. He took the bag and lifted it to his mouth when the man gestured encouragement. The relief to his throat made him want to cry.

As he drank, the man fingered the fine fringe of Jim's shirt. He touched his own cheek and raised his eyebrows.

Jim made the sign of the Snakes.

At Jim's hand sign, the man furrowed his brow and reached up to retrieve his pouch.

Jim spread the moisture from his lips onto his cheeks. "Gracias."

The man didn't return his smile. Debt paid, he walked away.

Finally accepting defeat, the Greys gave up hounding Fannin and sat scattered and dejected about the camp. Spohn's eyes followed the roaming Mexican soldiers as they mocked the vanquished or ran their hands over the muddy rifles. Other soldados cast nervous glances at the men who had killed so many of their fellows. Spohn's red eyes brimmed with unshed, angry tears, but Noah only saw the ground between his knees. The cigar-smoking man paced, glowering. With the heaviness in the air, the smoke floated around his head.

At some point, though empty-handed, Mrs. Cash and her son had been allowed to return.

As Jim walked toward the hospital, he was suddenly blown to the ground. He lay stunned, his ears ringing, the pain akin to someone jabbing something deep into his right canal. Briefly, incongruously, he remembered an icepick from his boyhood in Tennessee — the old handle had given him a splinter once.

Feet ran around him. After a moment, he sat up. He pawed his chest and picked out the chunks of wood embedded in his buckskin. Flames licked the splintered ammunition cart, and a blackened body lay on the ground next to other unburned corpses.

Daniel shouted in Jim's face, but he couldn't hear anything above the ringing. When he could stand, the mood of the camp had shifted to suspicion. Enraged soldados yelled commands and aimed their muskets at the prisoners. The Texians crouched with their hands in the air. Halfway down the prairie, officers struggled to control their spooked horses. At the same time, Ward and thirty of his men appeared on the horizon, too late and too few to help. They turned tail and ran, the Mexican cavalry on their heels.

Jim's hearing came back in a sudden rush during the roll call, as if his head had been under a waterfall, but Daniel answered for him. By process of elimination, Fannin declared the culprit to be Edward Isaac Johnson, the charred, moaning remnant of the cigar-smoking man. Not being one of the Greys, Jim hadn't bothered to learn his name before that. A Mexican officer borrowed one of his men's muskets. He twisted the bayonet and spat on Johnson before yanking it out.

"If the lid had been locked, the blast would have gone out instead of up," Daniel said, reaching to pluck splinters from Jim's cheek. "We're lucky. Hold still." He pulled a sliver from Jim's eyelid. "How did that not go in your eye?"

Jim put fingers in his ears and wiggled, then grabbed his earlobes, worried his hearing would never be the same after yesterday and today. Blood covered one of his fingertips.

Chapter 13

Eva

El Copano

At the bugle call, Eva turned toward the sloping canvas to hide her bruised face. After some convincing the night before, Pump had complied with her request and walloped her a good one. Tophe leaned over her, and she deepened her breathing. In the early morning chill, steam puffed from her lips.

"I can tell you are like the possum," Tophe whispered in English.

"It's called 'possuming.'" Eva's heart raced as she pulled the scratchy blanket higher. Tophe didn't make mistakes in English.

He switched to Spanish. "Wish I could sleep past the bugle call."

She grinned, eyes still closed. "Have a nice day," she said in a lazy voice.

Tophe grunted; then, she heard him buttoning and adjusting his uniform.

"Any luck with him?" he asked, referring to Pump's conversion. The cot creaked under his weight as he tugged on his boots.

"Yes. I'll get him to come around."

"Good." He left without another word.

Eva waited until she was sure he wouldn't return and sat up. She scrubbed her nails over her scalp and yawned. At full stretch, Eva winced and tested her puffy cheek with light fingers. She would wear her hair down today.

Her nausea was less this morning, and she mumbled a prayer of thanks to whomever was listening. So far, Tophe hadn't seen her vomit. After breaking her fast, she went in search of Francisca.

Francisca cast worried glances at her bruise as they walked, just as Eva had hoped. They followed a crowd to the wharf to see the schooner that had arrived. No ship had been scheduled.

Eva found it more challenging than she'd expected to make small talk with her. On every other mission, Eva spent this day with the officers' wives. There hadn't ever been a need to form a relationship with Francisca. Whenever she started to say something, she would see other wide-eyed Franciscas reaching out to her as Tophe beat them and then strangled them. What she wanted to say was, "Sorry for murdering you so many times. Can we be friends?"

When they reached the landing, Eva read the boat's name out loud. "The *William and Frances*. I wonder if it's an American ship or a British one?"

"I'm sure it must be American. I don't think British ships come to the Copano," Francisca said. "There's nothing here. I mean, look at what they're calling a wharf."

Eva laughed. "Perhaps it's intended to be aspirational?"

"Come. Let's get closer," Francisca said.

As they threaded their way single file through the curious onlookers, Eva placed a hand on her new friend's back.

On the deck, soldiers aimed muskets at the foreign sailors. One man argued furiously with Captain Jimenez. At the Mexican officer's order, two soldiers slung their firearms on their shoulders and restrained the angry man. No sailor ran for a weapon to defend or resist, and all remained still with their hands raised. The rest of the soldiers barked at the sailors and herded them off the ship.

Since the officers' wives didn't leave their tent to investigate, Eva had never witnessed this event before.

Tophe stood a distance away, and sensing her gaze, he turned to her. "Why are you out here?" he mouthed.

She kept her cheek turned away and shrugged. When he frowned and walked toward her, Eva's heart skipped a beat, but he changed course at a call behind him and went back to the warehouse.

An audible breath escaped from Francisca. "My husband has been angry with me, too. I can't seem to do anything right," she said. "Does he hit you often?"

"More since we arrived here," Eva said.

Francisca pursed her lips. "Telesforo only hit my face once. He was very sorry afterward." She took Eva's hand and squeezed it.

"He shouldn't hit you at all," Eva said. Though she wanted to speed-track Francisca's trust through sympathy and solidarity, she couldn't help her genuine thoughts from leaking through.

"Well, I think it must be the rare man that doesn't hit his wife occasionally."

Eva studied her new friend's profile as the prisoners marched by them. Francisca said those words as if they were true. Would she hear her if Eva told her the other officers didn't beat their wives?

In the evening, Eva sent a note to Tophe that she wasn't feeling well and would be eating in the tent.

When he came to check on her, he hissed when he saw her face. "What happened? It looks like you got punched."

"A private was running through camp on an errand, and we rounded the same corner. This was his shoulder. We both ended up on the ground."

Tophe's eyes widened. "Ouch. I'd take you to the doctor, but we don't have one."

"Yes, Santa Anna likes his troops to travel light," she said, remembering that detail from the Lux Libera scouting report and simultaneously recognizing what it meant for the soldiers. "It's okay. It's just a bruise."

"Are you sure your cheekbone isn't cracked?" He reached up to examine the bone underneath.

Eva flinched. "Don't. I felt it earlier, and nothing seemed to be broken. I think my face would be more swollen if it were cracked."

Continuing to examine her, he grimaced and wagged his head. "It's pretty swollen." He met her eyes. "It's good you won't be at dinner. The other officers will think I beat you. That's going to take a while to heal."

Eva pressed her lips together and nodded.

"Well… it won't matter after tomorrow night, anyway," he said. "I'll bring you back something to eat."

With a brief kiss to her forehead, Tophe left the tent.

"Eva?" Pump called from outside an hour later.

She rose from the cot where she had fallen asleep and peered out. "What are you doing here?" she asked as he entered. "I thought you had jumped to Louisiana."

"I found my wife. She was traveling with one of my sons, and they were still on the road." Pump sounded as if he'd run the entire way back. "Jim was attacked in San Felipe. A mob tried to lynch him, but he was saved by Daniel Allen."

At his words, Eva sank onto her bed. "But he's okay?" Her hands shook, and she clasped them in her lap.

Pump knelt in front of her. "Yes. Jane said he didn't receive any injuries that wouldn't heal."

"Where is he now?" she asked. "I should go to him."

"Jane couldn't remember which militia Daniel said he was joining up with, and Peter had been knocked out. She said too much happened at once. She was too concerned about Jim to pay attention to what was being said."

"So, he could be anywhere?" She wrapped her hands around her temples.

Pump cupped her knee. "I'm going to check Goliad first in the morning. Then I'll jump to where I think other militias might be. Houston should be in retreat and headed back to San Felipe." He shook his head. "I have to think like Daniel. I don't know what possessed him to join up. He's against the revolution." He touched her cheek, grimacing at the state of her bruise.

Eva stood but didn't know where to go.

Pump pushed himself off the ground. "You need to stay here and stick with the plan. It's the right choice. Jim's tough. He'll be all right."

She opened her mouth to argue just as Tophe stepped through the tent opening. When he saw Pump, he froze, plate in hand. Pump returned his stiff nod, and Tophe handed Eva the food.

In her imagination, her thoughts flew over the prairie, searching town by town, militia by militia, as she stared at the dish, but didn't see it.

"What's wrong?" Tophe asked.

His words jerked her to the present, and Eva shuttered. "Nothing. Sorry. Pump just woke me from a nap."

Stiffly, the two men traded places in the tent. Pump held Eva's eye and made to leave.

"I hope you consider returning to Lux Libera with us," Tophe said to his back. "For Eva's sake." His ominous tone shrank the tent.

Pump paused without looking back, peering into the darkness. "I'm considering it very carefully."

Chapter 14

Jim

Battle of Coleto

The defeated men buried their dead in the trenches. Fatigue made the work even harder.

In a booming voice over their heads, Mexican Colonel Holzinger announced the plan to leave the wounded on the field until they could be retrieved later with carts.

"They'll kill them when we're gone," Spohn said.

Daniel's brow creased with worry for Will. Jim didn't think they had anything to be concerned about, yet he followed when his friend nodded his head toward the hospital. They counted to three and lifted the boy together. Will groaned, still unconscious.

Two hundred armed soldados lined the road back to Goliad, and the two hundred and fifty Texians who could still walk under their own power stood double file, with the Greys leading the way.

As Jim and Daniel took their places, a Mexican lowered his bayonet in front of them. The man pricked Will's shirt and gestured for them to return him to the wounded. Daniel's temper flared, but Jim hauled him around, and they gently laid Will on his blanket. His brother-in-law rested a hand on his chest, but couldn't bring himself to leave the boy's side.

Others hovered over good friends and relatives, but Pettus waved his volunteers away. No one was very concerned about Fannin. From his pallet, the Colonel reassured the men of Urrea's good intentions and promises to intercede with Santa Anna on their behalf. "Dr. Barnard will be allowed to stay with the wounded," he said. "Dr. Field will go with you to Goliad."

More bayonets appeared in their faces. As Jim pulled Daniel to his feet, shouts of "¡Ándale!" rang in their ears.

Snare drums marked the time for their plodding feet on the dull march back to the fort. Ehrenberg whispered German curses in a steady stream only Jim could hear because the boy was directly behind him.

When they reached the San Antonio River, they rushed the banks. The water came up to their armpits, and they drank as they waded. Jim forced himself not to swallow too much and cautioned the men around him to do the same. Only Daniel listened to him. Spohn turned and stared at him like he was crazy. The prisoners waiting their turns shouted for them to hurry up and just cross already.

"¡Cállate!" the soldados shouted back.

Noah jogged up the muddy slope and slid an inch for every two he climbed. Jim put his hand down too soon, and Spohn trod on it when he stumbled.

At the pain, Jim hissed, and the soldier marching next to them laughed. Water drained from the hole in Jim's moccasin. When twilight reduced the day further to golden light with no heat, they shivered in their soaked clothes.

Before they saw it, they smelled Goliad. Smoke still trickled from the wattle-and-daub jacales they had torched before leaving. Mexican army tents spread from the walls in neat rows and columns across the prairie, and cook fires dotted the avenues. When he smelled the food, Jim's stomach rumbled loud enough for Daniel to hear, and his mouth flooded with saliva.

"Now I'm hungry," Spohn said, then flinched when the soldier marching next to him feinted a punishing blow.

At the south wall sally port, an officer called them to a halt. The setting sun cast long shadows from the presidio walls. No Mexicans seemed to have stepped foot within the gates since they had taken it, and the leading officer urged the prisoners forward. Some soldados studied their prisoners' reactions to the command, and others peered into the parade ground as if something were about to happen.

"They must think we laid mines before we left," Ehrenberg said.

Jim thought of the holes in the earth Europeans liked to dig and glanced back at the German.

In answer to Jim's confusion, the boy said, "Buried explosives. When you walk on them, BOOM." He made a quiet explosion with his mouth and opened his hands in an expanding circle.

Suddenly, Jim received a musket stock in the ribs for looking backward and fell into Daniel, but Ehrenberg defiantly whistled into the air as he sauntered past the guards and through the gate.

When the unexploded prisoners demonstrated the way to be clear and safe, their guards flanked them once again and herded them toward the chapel.

"Hey," Spohn said, smiling, "pays to be first in line. We're going to have a roof over our heads tonight."

Jim relaxed, happy at the thought of food, lying down on the dirt floor, and sleeping straight through until morning. As he passed through the doorway, the odor of burned beef and corn hung heavy in the air, so thick he could taste it.

The walls at the rear of the church were scorched midway to the vaulted ceiling, and the men stopped before the mound of gray ash until they were compelled up onto it. Jim, Daniel, and Ehrenberg put their backs to the wall. Ashes covered their feet to the ankle, and a man Jim knew only by sight pressed his behind to Jim's front. Jim braced his hands against the man's back, and the stranger mumbled an apology.

The soldados barked orders and swung their bayonets. From Jim's elevated position, he could see the rest of the prisoners streaming in without stopping.

"Are they putting all of us in here?" Noah asked. "We won't all fit. There's no way."

One soldier thrust and jabbed his bayonet down the center of the chapel where an aisle should be, forcing the men to pack tighter on either side and clearing a path. Jim shuffled to the right, and his neighbor's shoulder pressed his own up against his ear. When the soldier turned away, the men filled the aisle once again. A word from his fellow infantryman sent the man to clear the way again. More than one prisoner received a cut from his bayonet. Finally, in frustration, the soldier shot his musket into the air. Men ducked as debris rained down.

"He wants us to leave the path free," Spohn called out.

The soldier glared back in Spohn's direction, but all eyes dropped. The soldier took a step closer. "¿Quien habla español?"

When the man repeated the question in a calmer voice, Spohn raised his hand. Jim debated with himself before lifting his own, and the soldier motioned for them both to come to the aisle. Prisoners cursed and shifted to make room for them to pass.

Spohn reached the soldier first and darted fear-rimmed eyes at Jim. When Spohn answered his interrogator, he stuttered, but Jim could tell he responded correctly. The soldier jerked his thumb over his shoulder. After a moment's hesitation, Spohn looked back at his friends before striding down the aisle and out the chapel door. Now it was Jim's turn.

In rapid fire, the soldier shot questions at him, and Jim caught bits and pieces. He understood the gist of the questions, but his mind blanked. As quickly as he could, he flipped through the words in his memory, stopping and discarding them.

"Perdón, señor. Repita, por favor."

The soldado scowled at him and pushed him away with the stock of his musket. Jim tripped over the man behind him and opened his mouth to protest, but he had lost the soldier's attention. When communicating with his Mexican captives, Jim had never struggled for words. He just needed a moment to collect his thoughts. Jim's chest tightened as he threaded a path back to Daniel and Ehrenberg. Prisoners refused to move for him until he shoved his shoulder between them and forced his way to the wall.

"Nice try," Ehrenberg said.

Jim ignored him, his cheeks burning.

A bonfire illuminated the small courtyard just outside the front doors, and they heard Mexicans rolling two cannons up the ramp. Once in position, they pointed them at the prisoners with two soldados holding lit torches.

"They're not fucking around, are they?" Noah said. He stood nearby, sandwiched between two men to Jim's left.

Ehrenberg chuckled. "They're right to be afraid of us."

The door remained open, and soldados took turns pacing up and down the aisle.

Once all the prisoners settled into position, they were able to spread out an inch or two. The smallest men crouched where they were or laid themselves across their neighbors' feet. Others came to agreements on who would lie on top of whom or arranged themselves back-to-back. The wounded were given preference as much as possible.

A growing stench followed the sounds of vomiting and diarrhea from a few of the prisoners. Noah vomited all the water he had drunk at the river, and Jim gazed up at the ceiling, breathing through his mouth. When the soldados swapped with their brothers inside the chapel, they placed handkerchiefs over their noses.

"I'm sorry, fellas. I can't hold it any longer." Ehrenberg turned to piss on the wall, giving the permission they all needed to relieve their bladders. Jim ignored his sodden feet. He thought he would have suffocated if the ceiling hadn't been so high and the lofty windows didn't bring in a breeze from the door.

"When are they going to feed us?" Daniel asked.

Nobody responded, though the mood shifted. Daniel's question echoed through the ranks of prisoners, and the soldados stared blankly ahead.

"At least give us water," a man said.

Others took up the cry, including Jim, until the walls rang with "Agua!" Those tending to the wounded called for Dr. Field to be brought. Their pleas only hardened the faces of the soldados.

Out of pure exhaustion, the prisoners fell silent. Jim leaned against the wall, and the man in front of him leaned back against him. Jim closed his eyes and tried to sleep, but his mind drifted in and out.

Scuffles from the aisle roused him. At gunpoint, the Mexicans took blankets away from the wounded prisoners they could reach. Desperately, comrades tried to defend their helpless neighbors, and the rest of the chapel renewed begging for water. A soldier fired his musket.

"Shut up, you ungrateful, murdering thieves!" he bellowed in Spanish. "Dirty heretics. We should have executed all of you on the field."

"What did he say?" Ehrenberg asked.

"For us to shut up," Jim said.

The night passed with frequent choruses for water, but Jim didn't bother to join them and kept his eyes sealed. He thought he knew the game their captors were playing. Eva entered his thoughts, but Jim slammed the door on her. He didn't want her in this place.

At dawn, six men were allowed to fetch water from the river. The first load disappeared before it made it to the back of the chapel.

"Like a drop on a hot stove," Ehrenberg said to no one in particular. The thought made Jim thirstier.

By the third load, the dippers reached them on the back wall. They drank their fill and wanted more.

No food came for breakfast, but the men organized a new rotation for sitting and standing. Jim found the floor suffocating and gave his turns away before they were over.

In the evening, they were allowed to go for water again, and he guzzled his portion while Ehrenberg flexed his fingers at the gourd, waiting greedily. Angry prisoners cried out for food, but no one delivered supper. The soldados closed the chapel doors on their prisoners for the night.

Chapter 15

Eva

El Copano

Briefly, the sun shone down on El Copano. Eva wasn't sure she would ever dry out. She had spent the morning with Francisca, relaxing into a new friendship and enjoying the warmer weather. She could easily forget they could never truly be friends. But now, they stood near the open area where the recent prisoners, the men taken from the *William and Frances,* were being guarded. Seventy-five men sat hunched in the mud with their arms bound behind their backs. Purple to the elbow, their swollen hands puffed out from their hips.

Francisca gasped at the mistreatment, and Eva followed her as she confronted the sergeant. "What have these men done that they deserve to be tied this way?"

The sergeant blinked at her. "They are a U.S. militia that intended to join the rebels. We're waiting for the final order. Until then, they can sit as they are."

Francisca's lip curled, and she measured the length of the sergeant with the tip of her nose. Without another word, she strode toward the prisoner they had seen arguing with Captain Jimenez on the ship's deck.

"Madam!" the sergeant shouted after her.

She whipped around and put her face in the officer's. "Do you know who I am?"

The soldier swallowed and shifted his gaze over her shoulder, breaking eye contact. When he didn't answer, she continued across the yard.

"Who are you?" she asked the prisoner in English.

The man raised his head from his chest. His hair clung to his skull, wet and greasy. "My name is William Parson Miller, and I am Commander of the Nashville Battalion."

After hearing his accent, Eva thought, You're a long way from Ireland, Mr. Miller.

"And did I see you surrender without resistance yesterday?" Francisca asked.

"That would be so, ma'am." He coughed, his swallow catching in his throat.

She pivoted on her heel. At sight of her approach, the sergeant shrank. The other privates surrounding the prisoners hid smiles.

Before she reached him, she pitched her voice loud enough for the entire camp to hear, pointing a finger behind her. "As I witnessed myself, these men did not take up arms against Mexico. I insist you loosen their bonds."

The sergeant straightened. "I'm sorry, madam, you'll have to speak to Colonel Vara."

"Colonel Vara ordered you to cut off the circulation in their arms?" She tipped her head to the side, acid on her tongue. "I didn't say untie them; I said loosen them."

A muscle on the side of the sergeant's jaw ticked, but he jerked his head at the guards.

Francisca's eye traveled from soldier to soldier, then she called out, "And have these men been given any food or water since their surrender?" When no one answered her, she turned back to the sergeant.

Eva heard boots running closer and stepped aside to make room for the messenger.

"Colonel Vara orders the prisoners to be shot without delay." The boy panted, out of breath.

"No!" Francisca said. "Sir! The Mexican people do not murder prisoners of war."

The sergeant sneered. "You are correct, madam. Happily, these men are not prisoners of war, but opportunists and mercenaries. Those we do execute. Line up the prisoners!"

Francisca ran to the guards, urging them to ignore the order. The militiamen howled in pain and fought against the soldiers, who yanked them to their feet. They clustered in a protective huddle, begging for mercy or yelling defiant abuse, depending on the man.

"Madam, I don't care who you are," the sergeant shouted into Francisca's ear over the din, slicing the air with his hands. "You are interfering with us carrying out a direct order. These men do not deserve your sympathy. They're clearly criminals. We are *not* at war with the United States. They're not soldiers; they're ordinary citizens of a foreign nation who came here intending to harm us." With these words, he edged Francisca out of the way, and she ran to Eva's side.

Francisca grasped her hand and squeezed so tightly Eva thought her fingers would pop.

With bayonets, the soldiers prodded Miller's stubborn men into a tight line facing the bay, then paced back several yards to form the firing squad.

"Ready," the sergeant said. The soldiers lifted their muskets across their chests. "Aim." They brought them to their hips.

Francisca charged toward the prisoners, tugging Eva behind her, then released Eva's hand and threw her arms up. "Stop!" She built a shield with her body between the muskets and those doomed to die. "Colonel Vara!"

The sergeant put his hands on his hips, but the soldiers remained in position. At the spectacle of an officer's wife making a fool of herself, they tilted their heads and smirked at each other.

During the impasse, Francisca continued to call out, and Eva lent her voice. As the minutes lengthened and pooled in beaded coils, a crowd gathered, and Francisca's cheeks pinkened. The sergeant seemed to be debating the pros and cons of physically removing them.

Finally, Colonel Vara marched toward them, Tophe and Captain Alavez in his wake. "Madam Alavez, Madam Benavides, this is unseemly."

"Please, sir, have mercy on these men. They had not yet fought against us." Francisca lowered her arms. "Send them to Matamoros. They deserve a trial, at least."

Colonel Vara scanned the prisoners behind her.

In a low voice, she said, "Our president's decree is cruel and unjust. Please let me try to intercede with him. His wife, Inés, is to me as my own aunt."

After silent consideration, the creases around his mouth smoothed, and he consented. "I will do as you request," he whispered. Over his shoulder, he shouted the new commands.

"And please, sir," Francisca added, "I believe these men have been given no food or water since they arrived."

Colonel Vara scowled at the thought of sharing his supplies with the rebels.

"How would we want our own citizens treated, sir?"

He pursed his lips, sighed, and followed up his previous order with the additional one.

"Thank you, sir," she said, taking his hand.

He gave her a tight smile and set his free hand over their clasped ones. "Now, madam, please, leave my men to do their duty. I want no more interference."

When he passed their husbands on the way back to the warehouse, he stopped to converse with them, face hard. Tophe and Telesforo glanced at their wives simultaneously. The Colonel chopped the space between them to punctuate his disapproval, and Telesforo bowed his head, his hands placating. With their commander's parting injunction, both snapped to attention and saluted.

Francisca took Eva's hand and laced their fingers.

Telesforo and Tophe stomped toward them. Another officer distracted Tophe with a question, causing him to pause on the path. When Telesforo reached them, he hauled Francisca away, and Eva took the opportunity to disappear.

Later, when she thought Francisca might be alone in her tent, she crept along the side, listening. Telesforo's muffled, angry voice filtered through the canvas. Francisca apologized and soothed. Eva heard two dull strikes, followed by two more, and silence.

Eva peeked around the corner and saw Telesforo walking back to the warehouse. She knew he would spend the evening at cards in this line, but in the True line, he would make a different choice and return after dark, half-drunk and propelled by a humiliation he couldn't ignore.

"Francita," she called.

The tent flap opened. "Evita," Francisca said, smiling. Her face was puffy with unshed tears, but otherwise clear. Without another word, Francisca pulled her inside.

"I don't feel safe sleeping in my tent tonight," Eva said. "My father has left for Mexico City, and his tent is empty. Let's move our cots in there."

Francisca's forehead creased, and she put a finger to her chin, peering down at her bed.

"Just until our husbands' tempers have cooled," Eva added.

"Yes, all right, then… though let's leave a note telling him *you're* scared, and I'm comforting you for the night. I'll find someone to carry our things."

With a furtive retrieval of her cot and a short parade of baggage later, they were settled.

"I thought your father's tent was closer to your own," Francisca said.

Eva scrunched her nose. "It was the first place I knew Tophe would look for me. I had it moved." She glanced around to see if they had forgotten anything. She needed to make one last run to the latrine. "I'll be right back," she said, touching her knife. With one foot out the door, she paused. "If Tophe comes, you should run and hide."

Francisca's eyebrows shot up.

"In fact, here…." She retrieved her pistol from under the blanket and loaded it. When Eva placed it in her hand, Francisca pinched the handgrip.

"Have you fired a pistol before?"

Francisca shook her head.

Eva took it back from her and demonstrated how to hold it safely. "This is half-cock… this is full-cock. You need full-cock. It's already primed and loaded. Shoot him in the foot. Or better, above your head," she said. "But don't hesitate, and then you need to run. If he's in the way, push through with your shoulder. He won't be expecting you to do any of that."

Francisca's face wrinkled in disbelief, and she laughed.

Eva frowned. "I'm serious."

"But why would he hurt me?"

Good question, Eva thought. "Because he's angry you involved me today. He thinks your husband needs to do a better job keeping you in line. If he is looking for me and finds you, he might beat you to find out where I am." She pointed at her cheek. "And he doesn't avoid faces."

Her amusement fading, Francisca bit her lower lip, and Eva felt safer about leaving her alone. When she exited the tent, she pulled out her knife and glanced over her shoulder. It was a long walk to the other side of the grove, and she sped up her pace, nearly jogging.

At the last tree, Tophe appeared from behind it and casually leaned against the trunk.

Eva halted in her tracks.

A nearby torch illuminated half his face as he arched an eyebrow. "What's going on, Eva?"

"I'm not going to let you kill Francisca," she said. "But I need to pee really badly."

He pointed his chin toward the latrine, and as she brushed past him, he said, "This was the one place I knew you'd have to turn up at some point. You seem to need to go all the time now."

Even though her pregnancy was hardly showing, her body had been making surprising demands. The clues were there if Tophe knew how to read them, Eva thought with a shiver of dread. When she returned, she was able to think straight again.

"You know, the youngest of the men Francisca saves go on to be Confederate officers defending an unjust economic system," he said. "If you truly think this world is not a shadow, why would you want to save them?"

Eva had forgotten. Was it right to save them? Could an entire life be reduced to the rightness or wrongness of later decisions? "But not in every line. Sometimes they make different choices. We can't know what they will choose in this line's future. Francisca is making the right choice now. That's what matters." She took a step toward him. "We've saved Lincoln from assassination countless times, but in many timelines, he hangs thirty-eight starving Dakota rebels whose people had been told to eat grass the same week he signs the Emancipation Proclamation. Often, he is harsher throughout his second term. In others, he honors the treaties the United States made with the Tribes. We have to let people make their own choices. We can't predict."

"No, that's why we must match the True line. You know this, Eva! You're over-complicating things."

"Why is Axis Mundi the only real one? It still contains humans making choices out of love or survival or greed. Only we can see the outcomes of all the decisions, but even that's an illusion. All of them spin off into a capillary of branching paths. We can't see into the heart of a soul as it moves through the network. Everything is probable and just a probability. The path exists because it must, but the soul doesn't have to choose to walk down it. Should a person be judged by anything other than their choice in the moment?"

"It's fate, Eva! They have no choice," Tophe said.

"I don't believe that. Not anymore," she said. "We shouldn't be the Editors of the multiverse's arena, choosing, like the Romans, who lives and who dies with the turn of a thumb, taking our cues from the fickle crowd of Elders. How do they even know the real history of the True line? None of us can move through the fourth dimension there! Including our leaders!"

Tophe placed his forehead in his palm. "You're not making any sense. It's like we're not even speaking the same language."

"Other people's choices narrow our own until we have none. Fate only comes into play when we bump up against the consequences of other people's decisions. But when we can, we still choose for ourselves. Who are we to try to kill God, to contain God, to silence God?"

Tophe squeezed his eyes shut against her blasphemy. "No… that's not… You can't…." He covered his face and shook his head. After a moment, he froze and dropped his hands. "Who gave you that bruise?"

"Pump."

As if seized by an epiphany, his mouth cracked open, and his eyes glittered. "I have never lied to you. Never betrayed you, even when our Elders required it," he said, pain in his voice. "You're the only person I've ever really cared about. We have always trusted each other with everything. I would give my life for you! Why? Why have you been lying to me?"

"I believe Pump. I've seen things Lux Libera has intentionally hidden from us. And why?" she asked.

"Why have they been hidden from us? I can't erase the horrible things we've done, but I can stop the next one."

Tophe shoved off from the tree and broadened his shoulders. Eva took a step back.

"Are you afraid of me now?" he asked, moving farther into the light.

"No. I don't want to hurt you."

"Hurt me? You *are* hurting me. It will kill me to see you cleansed and marked and then know you will be trapped forever in darkness!"

"I can't be Lux Libera anymore, Tophe." The words Eva feared to say pushed at her tongue. "I love my husband. My real husband." Blood rushed in her ears, and her breath quickened. She rolled the hilt of the knife in her hand. "I'm pregnant with his child."

Tophe's face contorted as his mouth fell open.

"Stay in this world with me," she said, her vision blurring. "Don't return. We can be free to travel where we want. Pump showed me how to skim timelines. I can show you how to jump from anywhere, any distance." Light-headed, she scanned his face for his reaction.

He just stared at her as the air shifted between them. "Where's Pump?"

"Gone."

When he advanced, she raised her knife. He stopped and put up his hands.

"I love you," Eva said, letting the tears fall. "Will you leave Lux Libera and stay with me?"

"No," he said without hesitation. He set his jaw; his eyes focused on her. He took another step toward her.

Invisible in the darkness, she tucked her free hand behind her back, formed a portal, and slipped through.

Chapter 16

Eva

In the deep shadows outside Pump's tent, Eva exited the portal, sank where she stood, and wept. Her teeth bit into the palm of her free hand to keep Francisca from overhearing, and she drove her knife into the mud. After a time, she straightened her legs and dried her eyes. Just as she heard a footstep behind her, she felt the point of a muzzle dig into the back of her head. It pressed deeper as he pulled back the flint with a click.

With her hands in the air, she let the knife fall and turned. "Please, Tophe…"

"Menik'esak'esi āyasifeligimi," a female voice said.

Shocked, Eva froze and ran the foreign words through her head. They sounded like Amharic.

"Sorry, let's try German," the strange woman said. "I don't want us to be understood if we're overheard. Where's your partner?"

"May I turn around?"

"Slowly."

Eva rotated in place. The woman's face was a black hole in the dark, and Eva tried to identify her voice. "Ingabire?" she asked, naming another Mender she knew, but not well.

"Don't make me ask you again."

After studying her for another moment, Eva felt certain she didn't recognize her. She debated between lies. "I don't have a partner. I'm working this mission alone." Upon further thought, she tucked her chin in confusion. "Why are you pointing a gun at me?"

The woman ignored her. "We saw you arrive with him. We know he left two days ago. Where did he go?"

She must mean Pump, Eva thought. "Who are you?"

"Answer my questions, please."

Fear crept up Eva's throat, but she swallowed it back down. "What's your mission here?" A duplicated assignment would explain the second beacon. "I think the scouts, or the strategists, must have made a mistake." When the woman still didn't respond, Eva took a step forward, and the stranger retreated a single pace. Eva extended a hand. "If you're here to kill the Angel of Goliad, I won't let you. I have no desire to hurt you."

The woman laughed. "We know you're here to kill her."

"Of course," Eva said. "But I'm not going through with it. Who's your target?"

"You."

Eva's stomach lurched, and she braced herself to be shot. They knew. Somehow, they knew. Tophe's voice echoed in her ears. What is time to Lux Libera? Her chest ripped open at the thought of her true friend betraying her. No, not possible. She shoved the thought away and calculated if she could wrestle the pistol from her or had time to create a portal. "Am I your only target?"

"Your partner, too."

Sheer terror scratched fingers down her back. She must have meant Tophe and not Pump. Everyone knew their association. "My partner is still loyal to Lux Libera. I'm the only one who should be punished."

"Put your hands back up." Courage seemingly restored, the woman reclaimed her original ground. "Lux Libera, is it? That's a new one for me."

Eva's racing mind screeched to a halt. "Wait. I don't understand. Who are you?"

"T'ibek'a. I come from a long line of Tebakiyochi, and we are the Guardians of timelines. We don't let other travelers do things to change them."

"*You're* the second beacon," Eva said, pointing a finger.

"Ah, ah, ah… hands." The stranger gestured with the pistol. "Yes. We arrive before large events and patrol. Our entry points can serve doubly as traps, and we like to plant false ones. We also remove enemy beacons if we find them. We replaced the one we found here in El Copano with one set several days earlier. Those are my favorite. It's like moving someone's bookmark without them knowing." The woman chuckled, then cocked her head to the side. "I saw you fall, you know. We're always prepared for the possibility of an uninvited guest arriving at our beacon. I thought you were dead."

Eva shivered, remembering that night. "You kill your targets?"

"Not ideally. Our goal is to take them back with us and, after a fair trial, throw them into the Abyss."

"I've never heard of you."

"And Lux Libera is a new one for me. I will report your existence when I return. There are many groups who believe they are the only ones." The woman lowered her weapon, and Eva chanced a look over her shoulder to see if she had been flanked. Without warning, the Guardian tossed the pistol in her hand to grasp the barrel and struck Eva on the temple.

When Eva woke, she lay on a bare concrete platform cantilevered from the wall. A desk and a toilet lined the opposite walls, and a narrow window beneath the ceiling allowed brilliant natural light to bathe the room. If she hadn't known better, she would have thought she was in Penance Hall.

Her head throbbed, and she worried about her ability to travel. Further thoughts of losing Jim alarmed her. Without rising, she arranged her hands and listened for the chorus of strings. Relieved she could still hear it, she took a breath and sat up, bracing against the imaginary pickax gravity stabbed into the side of her skull.

As she hung her head until the pain subsided, she noticed the hems of her skirts were wet, and sand covered her boot heels. She gathered the cloth and squeezed out a stream of seawater onto the hard floor. For another moment, she rested and then took a deep breath.

Between her hands, motes of light danced in the sunbeam. The effort to re-tune the particles' strings jabbed needles behind her eyeballs, but she slowly looped each snippet one by one until, clef by clef, the layers of the symphony began to sing the song she needed. Before she could complete the portal, the lock on her door turned with a mechanical thud.

She closed her hands, and the hazy pool dispersed in a puff.

Her captor and a new man entered the room.

"Please," Eva said. "Where am I?"

"The sacred city of Lalibela," the woman said.

"Ethiopia?"

"Yes. Turn and put your hands behind your back."

The man cuffed Eva, and they led her out of the cell and down a narrow corridor. Outside, Eva glanced around a beautiful campus much like the sanctum, though the landscape reminded her more of the Big Bend Country of her own birth line in Texas than the ancient ash forest of Axis Mundi in the True line's Germany.

Tall, circular buildings stretched around the horizon and reminded her of beehives. Closer in, decorative fountains filled each courtyard, and the aromas of roasting coffee and frankincense hung in the air.

As they passed a deep quarry in the ground, Eva realized an entire two-story building had been hewn from the living rock beneath their feet. She peered over the edge to study the carvings, but they turned down a sidewalk, and it was lost from sight.

They entered a cool breezeway, and the man pulled her into an interrogation room. After handcuffing her to the table, her captors seated themselves across from her.

The man tugged a flat television screen toward himself. Eva marveled at a technology she had never seen before and wondered how far into the future they were compared to Lux Libera. Pump had encouraged her to explore forward beyond her own time, but she hadn't built up the courage yet. She found her old taboos hard to shake.

"My name is Ephrem, and this is Kidisti," he said in German. "Which language do you prefer to be questioned in?"

"English."

"Name?"

"Eva."

"Full name, please."

"Lux Libera only uses first names. I relinquished my middle and family name when I took my vows. I am forbidden from speaking them." As she uttered the words, she realized she was no longer bound by them.

"Tell us more about your organization," Kidisti said.

In the interest of efficiency, Eva opted for total honesty and described Lux Libera, their belief system, and their sacred mission. Her interrogators' faces darkened the longer she talked, and misgivings about her strategy curled through her gut.

Ephrem darted his eyes at Kidisti before drilling into Eva's. "Your cult is one of the most monstrous we've come across. How long have you been a follower?"

Eva dropped her gaze. "Please, sir, I left Lux Libera months ago. I was actually trying to protect the Angel of Goliad from my former partner."

He sniffed. "A liar, too, and a bad one at that. You could at least try to make eye contact."

Eva's head shot up. "I'm not lying!"

Ephrem's chair fell back as he reached across the table and slammed her head down, thankfully on the uninjured side. He brought his nose to hers. "How long have you been a follower?"

Panicked, Eva said, "Only a couple of years."

"That doesn't add up," Kidisti said. "You said you were taken when you were twelve. You're early twenties, at least."

Ephrem's hand pushed until stars sparked across her vision, and she cried out. He eased the pressure but kept her pinned.

"Ten or twelve years. It's hard to know when you've traveled as much as I have."

"Ten or twelve years as a… what did you call yourself? A Mender?" he asked. "You must have murdered thousands of people in that time. Caused tens of thousands of deaths." His fury lent weight to his arm, and Eva grimaced. "Throwing you into the Abyss myself will be a privilege."

"I was only a scout," she said. "I just got promoted." Even to her own ears, her terrified voice sounded wheedling.

"I don't believe that for a second." With a final shove, he released her and picked up his chair, but didn't sit back down. He rounded the table and hovered over her.

Eva concentrated on slowing her breathing, but her body refused to stop shaking. She discarded Lux Libera etiquette and forced her eyes to lock on her captor's. "I know it sounds far-fetched, but after I fell down your trap, I was rescued by a man who lived nearby. I came to understand his world was just as real as the True line, and everything Lux Libera had taught me was a lie. I renounced my vows and went to El Copano to stop my partner. I had hoped, still hope, to convince him of the truth."

Kidisti sat back in her chair, uncertain.

"Remember?" Eva said. "Remember what I said to you? I told you I wouldn't let you kill the Angel of Goliad. That I wasn't going through with it. I thought you were Lux Libera sent to assassinate me or take me back."

Her captor shifted her attention to Ephrem, who still stood centimeters from her shoulder.

"It's true. She said that to me."

Encouraged, Eva said, "I can't change what I've done, but I can protect Francisca. And if I can convince my partner to see the truth, I can protect many more people in the future."

Ephrem growled over her head. "The Abyss will do that for us once we arrest him. Less hassle."

In supplication, Eva opened her cuffed fists. "Please, Kidisti. Let me return. I can help you protect that timeline." She craned her neck to see Ephrem. "Your people seem to value life. Do you also value redemption? I was misled. I'm not a murderer." She twisted back to Kidisti. "I have skills you can use. I can speak many languages. I understand many cultures in different times."

Her captor held her stare for several seconds before she broke it off. After Kidisti touched a button on her television screen, she motioned for Ephrem to follow her outside. The door slammed behind them, and Eva strained her ears to decipher their muffled conversation through the heavy wood.

When they didn't return, she curled her thumb joint to her pinky and tried to pull her hand through the restraint, but he had left no wiggle room. She could form a portal, but she couldn't walk through it.

Maybe if she scooted through and took the table with her?

A tiny portal formed between her palms, and she expanded it by stretching her fingers to their full extent. She threw her torso against the table's edge, but it didn't budge. Looking down, she saw bolts fastening the legs to the floor.

Overcome with frustration, she jerked both arms, skinning her wrists in the process, and the portal disintegrated with the rattle of chains.

Chapter 17

Eva

Disheartened, Eva lowered her head to the tabletop and closed her eyes. She needed to think.

Moments later, the door opened, and Kidisti returned. After sitting, she tapped the television screen again and looked up expectantly. "Ephrem is bringing us food. Neither of us has eaten, and we can discuss your possible recruitment into T'ibek'a. In the meantime, I'd like you to list your skills for me. Please speak clearly." After Eva had named the languages she spoke and the worlds she had worked in, Kidisti quizzed her, switching languages mid-sentence and expecting her to keep up.

"So, never a mission in an Ethiopian or an Amharic world? You don't know any of our language?"

"No, but I'm a fast learner," Eva said. "I've heard it before, of course, but my strengths have always been in European languages."

Kidisti tilted her head. "I'm surprised. So many worlds speak Amharic as their primary language, even in their Europes. We are the birthplace of humanity and the Original timeline, after all." With a sigh, she shrugged. "We could use your talents, but my partner will be harder to convince. You have… quite a record. Of course, we will need to get final approval from the high council. If we don't, you'll have a trial, but based on your own testimony, your execution is guaranteed."

Eva gnawed at her lips, kicking herself for her naivety. She had thought convincing them of her good intentions would be simple. Instead, she had prejudiced them. She should have lied through her teeth.

Ephrem nudged the door open with his back and held a platter with both hands. When Kidisti uncuffed her, Eva rubbed her wrists and debated trying to escape. Ephrem set the platter between them on the table, and Kidisti eyed her curiously.

Eva realized this would be a test. A small one, but still a test. Rolls of tan, spongy flatbread rimmed the circumference of the platter, and dollops of stew and chunks of sauced meats soaked into a single layer of flatbread in the middle. Ephrem slipped back outside, retrieved a pitcher, a cloth, and a basin, laid them next to the platter, then settled to watch her.

Would the water be for washing after the meal or before? Eva studied the communal nature of the setting and the lack of utensils, made a decision, and stood to pour water over her hands. Ephrem's face remained impassive, but a smile played on Kidisti's lips. On a hunch, Eva offered to wash their hands, and they took turns letting her pour water over their palms and fingers. Ephrem handed her the cloth, and she sat back down.

Next, Eva sent her hand out above the stew and hovered over a piece of meat as she watched Kidisti's face. The corners of the woman's mouth drifted downward ever so slightly, and Eva shifted to a roll of flatbread. Take the whole thing or tear off part? she wondered. There was plenty for each person to have more than one, but it might look greedy if she held an entire roll in her hand. Eva split the difference, tore off a piece from the roll before her, and used it to scoop up a bite.

Kidisti's smile grew, and she and Ephrem tore squares off the same roll closest to them, bringing the piece to their lips for a kiss and touching it to their foreheads. Eva copied them on her following bite, and they ate in silence.

Entirely focused on surviving, Eva hadn't paid attention to how ravenously hungry she had been and, for the briefest of moments, relaxed as her belly filled. Soon, food coated her fingers, and Eva almost licked them before she caught herself. She noticed Ephrem wiping his fingers on a piece of bread as if it were a napkin and mimicked him.

Without warning, Kidisti leaned forward with a bite in her hand and brought it next to Eva's mouth. Eva considered if she should refuse ritually or accept, but took a gamble and opened wide. Kidisti smiled and placed the tastiest tidbit into her mouth.

Stuffed, Eva wiped her fingers a final time and sat back in her chair.

When he finished eating, Ephrem crossed his arms over his chest and ran Eva through his own set of language tests and cultural trivia questions. After another hour of questioning, he turned to Kidisti and nodded. "I think she could be a potential asset. It's worth giving her a probationary period."

"Okay, here's the deal," Kidisti said. "Assuming we can get approval from the high council, you protect the Angel until Telesforo abandons her in Mexico City at the end of the war. You'll have until then to turn your partner to our cause. If you fail, we will arrest him. If you try to run, we will hunt you down. Hold out your arm."

"Why?" Eva asked as she complied.

Neither answered, but Ephrem removed a large, handled syringe from his jacket pocket.

Not liking the look of the instrument, Eva cringed back in her seat. "What is that?"

"This will insert a beacon. We will be able to track you wherever you go. If you try to remove it, it will send a signal to us."

Eva had never seen a beacon so small. "That can't possibly work."

As he ran the hollow needle under the skin near her inner elbow, Ephrem smirked. "Try to take it out. See what happens."

Eva grimaced as she stifled a pained cry.

"You have to earn our trust before we'll let you become a Tebaki," he said. "Until then, you'll be treated like the criminal you are. You have much to atone for, and the road to redemption will be long."

Blood dripped down the crease of her arm, and Eva contemplated his words. Maybe this was what she deserved. Was it right for her to quietly live out her days with Jim after all she had done? The thought tore her heart from her chest, and her hand covered the gaping hole it left. Maybe she could negotiate living with Jim while still serving them. He would feel no loss of time while she was gone.

The Guardians stood and motioned for her to stand and turn. They recuffed her and led her back to her cell.

Alone again, she paced. She reminded herself there was no urgency here. Jim's world remained frozen and unaffected by the passage of time in this Lalibela. The prudent course of action would be to wait for the verdict from the high council. With their blessing, she could continue with her plans, but if she ran now, she'd be trying to dodge their operatives, which might be impossible. If they decided to execute her, she'd escape to another world to remove the tracker. And then… return to Jim's world and do her best to keep everyone alive, including herself.

Unable to stand any longer, she finally settled on the bed and allowed herself to close her eyes. The best thing she could do while she waited was rest. The more she pushed herself, the more her pregnancy forced her body to rebel with unrelenting nausea and exhaustion.

They let her cool her heels for three days, and on the fourth, the lock turned on her door. Kidisti and Ephrem entered her room, and Kidisti said, "We have the approval of the high council."

Confused, Eva asked, "They didn't want to see me?"

"They reviewed your video," Ephrem said.

"Video? What video?" Eva shifted her attention back and forth between the two Tebakiyochi. "I didn't see a camera."

"Lux Libera is currently in 1997, correct?" Kidisti asked.

"Yes."

Ephrem scrunched a shoulder, mildly bored.

"We will be keeping an eye on you," Kidisti said. "Ephrem is positioned with Sam Houston's men, but we meet daily to report to each other. With you watching Goliad, I will be free to patrol other towns. Don't disappoint us."

Eva inclined her head and spoke from her heart, but left a loophole open. "I swear to protect Francisca Alavez. I swear to protect timelines." Though she might agree more with T'ibek'a's purpose than Lux Libera's, she didn't want to be another organization's sworn assassin. In an instant, her freedom had been snatched away again, and the thought chilled her. When she lifted her eyes, they evaluated each other for another moment.

Ephrem arched a doubtful eyebrow. "We'll see." He turned his face to his partner. "I need to resupply before I return to Houston's army. You go ahead with her. I'll see you at our rendezvous tomorrow. Usual time."

On their way out, he went his own way, but as she and Kidisti passed the sunken building again, Eva asked, "Is that one of the churches of Lalibela?"

"Yes," Kidisti said. "If and when you become a T'ibek'a Guardian, you will defend Lalibela, including its sacred churches. This sanctuary is only one of eleven. Our most honored Tebaki watches over the Ark of the Covenant in Aksum in the northern highlands, but the rest of us Tebakiyochi are stationed here or on missions protecting God's will in His timelines."

At the woman's words, Eva's heart recognized an instant spiritual kinship. She understood this believer's language well and could easily imagine a world in which she molded herself into a Tebaki's image. She shook herself, blindsided by her hunger and vulnerability. Renouncing Lux Libera had created an enormous hole in her soul, which now stood empty and cried out to be filled. Only self-awareness and her love for Jim kept her from converting on the spot. Instead, and genuinely curious, Eva said, "Many Ethiopias claim to hold the Ark of the Covenant. How do you know you have the real one?"

Kidisti frowned. "They're all real. This is God we're talking about."

Eva imagined what Pump would make of their theology. They seemed to think they had all the answers, just like Lux Libera.

Kidisti led her to the nearest fountain and took her hand. When she touched the water's surface, a portal spread, thick as rainbowed oil. "Ready?" she asked. "Just step in."

With a lift of her boot, Eva entered the portal, and Kidisti silently assumed control of her strings. Eva's breath caught, startled at the violation, and as they traveled between the worlds, she struggled to regain her composure. After a timeless moment, she found herself standing on the beach.

When she could speak, she asked, "Do you always travel through water?" Maybe she and Jim could move to one of the bands living on the parched, treeless Staked Plains.

"I can go through trees, too, but the fountains in Lalibela are more convenient." In the darkness, Kidisti's teeth shone as she regarded her ward. When she returned Eva's knife, she said, "Everyone deserves a second chance. Don't prove my partner right that some people are beyond redemption."

"I don't plan to."

They parted ways, and Eva followed the beach, listening to the surf in her ears. When she reached the tent where she had hidden Francisca, Eva braced herself for the questions she knew would come. An overwhelming desire for simplicity and homesickness for Jim consumed her, but Eva pulled the flap aside and ducked her head to enter. Her friend sat where she had left her.

"I was beginning to get worried; you were taking so long. Were you speaking German just now?" Francisca asked, then gasped. "What happened to your temple?"

"My husband," Eva said, sick to death of lies.

Chapter 18
Jim

Presidio La Bahía Goliad

The smelly fug of so many sick, injured, and unwashed men had nowhere to go and only thickened the stifling heat. Afraid to sleep for fear of smothering, Jim pressed his spine against the wall, but his body had other ideas, and he dozed despite his determination to stay awake.

Breakfast, again, consisted of water. When the doors closed without food appearing, the prisoners' rage boiled over. Fists banged on the entry.

"We capitulated!" "We were promised the same rations!" "Where is Urrea?" "Where is Holzinger?" "Where is Dr. Field?" The shouts devolved into a roar as enraged men pulled at the great handles and rattled the doors.

"I'd rather die trying to fight our way out than starve to death in here," Daniel said, forcing his way to the front.

Equally angry and ready to act, Jim followed him, but they didn't make it very far.

"That's what they want," Ehrenberg shouted. "If we start fighting, they'll have an excuse to gun us down right here and now."

Other prisoners came to the same sick realization. "Stop! Stop!" They shoved at the instigators to clear them and took their places in front of the door. Two men scuffled, neither able to draw back for a punch. Above the chaos, they heard the bar being removed and froze.

Sunlight streamed in, and Jim blinked at the silhouette of Mexican Colonel Holzinger flanked by four soldados, muskets lowered.

"Gentlemen," the Colonel said. "Please. Please. There is no food. Our soldiers. They have no food." He paused. "Ehrenberg, kommen bitte übersetzen."

Ehrenberg pushed his way to the front of the chapel and stood before the Colonel, a former fellow German, but now his enemy captor. After a long moment of conversing, he turned to face the prisoners. "Our gracious host assures me he is doing his utmost to drive up some steers to butcher for us. Their own soldiers have not had rations for two days. They have no provisions themselves."

The men grumbled at the blatant lie.

"I have promised we will be quiet until this evening," Ehrenberg said, and the muttering increased.

Holzinger withdrew, and the doors shut again. At the sound of the bar sliding into place, the prisoners who wanted to fight their way out cursed Ehrenberg.

"I promise you, fellas," he said. "If they don't bring food tonight, I'll be leading the charge."

That day crawled by just as miserably, though someone played their flute every few hours. If Jim knew the song, he mouthed the words.

More Texian wounded arrived on carts, and those poor souls were stuffed into the chapel with the ones who had come the day before. Will, Colonel Fannin, and the Greys' Captain Pettus numbered among the last group. Since the newcomers could only lie down, all organized rotations ceased, and Jim and the other unwounded men stood packed against each other. Daniel groused, stuck and unable to check on his brother-in-law.

"At least he's still alive," Jim said. "They wouldn't have bothered to bring a dead body."

That evening, the door opened again. Beef had been sent. The men cheered, and Jim's eyes teared. His stomach had stopped hurting hours before, but images of food intruded on every thought.

When his portion of meat made its way to him, he held a raw piece smaller than his fist. His companions stared at theirs in dismay and curled their lips in disgust when Jim began eating his immediately.

"What are we supposed to do with this?" Daniel asked. The blood dripped through his fingers.

"Eat it," Jim said. "Obviously."

Daniel puffed his cheeks.

Prisoners along the side walls pulled down the wooden panels of the Stations of the Cross and started two small fires.

"The Catholics aren't going to like that," Ehrenberg said.

Noah wrinkled his nose. "It'll take all night for everyone to cook their meat." The heat and smoke from the fires hung beneath the level of the windows.

"There's not enough wood," Jim said.

"Put those fucking fires out! You're gonna kill us all," someone said. "I can't fucking think it's so goddamn hot in here!"

"Better than freezing our balls off," Noah said.

"Is it?" Daniel asked. "Is it really?"

"Ah, Noah, ever the optimist," Ehrenberg said.

"I'm just saying… of the two."

"Well, you'll be comfortable in hell, then," Ehrenberg said. "I'm pretty sure this is a foretaste."

Daniel watched Jim lick his hand and between his fingers.

"It's not that bad," Jim said. "In fact, it's good. Don't think about it. Just eat." As he watched his friend nibble, his smile grew. "I'll eat it if you can't." Jim bared his teeth like a wolf as he imagined his fingers closing around the meat, but clasped his hands together instead. "Just eat it, damn it."

Daniel took a real bite, chewed, and swallowed.

Jim closed his eyes and tried to think of other things or sleep. He didn't care which. No water had accompanied the food, and the beef worsened his thirst. He wasn't sure he minded smothering to death anymore.

When the doors opened in the morning, fresh air rushed in. To Jim's surprise, the soldados commanded them to exit. He was handed a dipper of water when he passed through the door, and Jim gulped as much as he could before it was yanked from his grasp, then followed Daniel down the ramp. A soft, icy drizzle bathed him, and he inhaled clean air.

They were led to the open parade ground and an area encircled by armed guards. Noah and Jim laughed at each other as they opened their arms wide and tilted their heads back to catch the rain. Daniel lay down in the mud, uncaring. As the euphoria lapsed, Jim squatted beside him.

"Will didn't look good," Jim said, beginning to shiver. Once he had stopped moving, the wind cut through his buckskin.

Daniel cracked an eye. "No. At least it seems the wounded are staying in the church."

"Now that we're out here…." Jim gazed around at the bayonet-spiked human wall surrounding them. "Assuming they don't stuff us back in, we need to start planning our escape."

Chapter 19

Eva

El Copano

The next day, Eva didn't leave Francisca's side. Telesforo insisted his wife return to his tent, but the women convinced him to allow Eva to spend the night with them. She would sleep in her buffalo robe at the foot of Francisca's cot.

Uncomfortable with the arrangement, Telesforo informed Eva in the morning that he would be speaking with her husband on her behalf. It wasn't right that she was so afraid of him, he had said. He was a good man.

Yes, Eva had thought, he is. She wondered how the conversation had gone because Telesforo made no efforts to extract her that night, and Eva kept her head down. Whenever she thought of Tophe, her chest tightened, and she longed for the person she used to be.

Now, they traveled to Goliad in a column. Eva knew what awaited her once they reached the presidio in a few days. Fannin's ill-fated Texians would be imprisoned on the parade ground, miserable and exposed to the elements. The danger to Francisca from Tophe would only increase as he tried to stop her.

Miller's men from the *William and Frances* trudged ahead in three files, their hands tied to lead lines. With bayonets fixed, soldiers flanked them on both sides. Eva had secured Pump's horse to her own and rode with the baggage train amongst the officers' wives.

At midday, she hobbled her horse to graze and walked up the line, searching for Tophe. Camp followers spread blankets and laid out food. When he saw her waiting for him to notice her presence, he pretended not to have seen her and shifted his back in her direction. She sighed and marched to him. "May I speak with you, husband?"

Telesforo and Captain Jimenez stopped talking and looked up. Tophe stiffened. When the other officers excused themselves, he turned a stormy face toward her.

"What?"

She squatted beside him and glanced around. They would not be overheard if she kept her voice low. "After I left you, I was attacked by another traveler."

Tophe leaned away from her, confused. "What do you mean?"

"Apparently, there is an organization that guards timelines. They call themselves the T'ibek'a and patrol to catch people like us." She frowned. "Surprised me with a pistol to the back of the head."

"Second beacon," he said, his face relaxing at a mystery solved.

"Yes."

"Did they try to kill you?" he asked, scanning her body.

"No, she intended to arrest me, but then offered to recruit me."

"What happens after they arrest you?"

"Abyss."

Tophe nodded and puckered his lips. "Sure. Of course." He gazed at the middle distance with a bitter smile. "Fail to complete enough missions? Abyss," he said, waving his hand. "Heresy? Abyss. Fornication? Abyss. Now… *complete* a mission? Abyss?" He squinted at her. "Why are you telling me this? Wouldn't that solve your problem? Me in the Abyss?"

At the hate and betrayal in his eyes, she reared back in shock. "How could you think that, Tophe? After all we've been through? I'm telling you this because if I can recruit you, they will spare you."

"I don't need sparing. Or recruiting. I have a people. The True and only people. Thank you for clarifying who my enemies are, though."

"You're including me in that list?" she asked, pointing to herself. Her ribcage opened. Tophe could have plucked her beating heart if he had reached out a hand.

His eyes only darkened, and she stood up.

Presidio La Bahía Goliad

Four days of watching and plotting yielded no viable escape plans. Each drizzly day and torchlit night, alert guards thwarted every possibility. The loaded cannons pointed at them added to the security measures.

With nothing to do, Jim stared at his bare, mud-encrusted feet and hugged his knees. He had long since traded his moccasins with a Mexican soldier for food. Other men with cash in their pockets paid dearly. Those with blankets found no comfort in the sodden rags and traded them away.

But they were allowed to have fires sometimes, and when they got their hands on any meat, they cooked it. One day, they roasted the discarded hooves of a calf and ate them all.

Occasionally, they saw Spohn when he wasn't translating for the officers. Not being allowed to approach close enough to speak, Spohn passed them stale tortillas by way of the guards when he could. They quickly learned which soldados would drop them on the ground versus who would hand them over with bored looks on their faces.

Jim tightened the laces on his breechcloth and leggings. Daniel's thinning face sagged, and Jim rubbed his own, scratching the bristles on his cheek.

Sometimes, the men would sing "Home, Sweet Home" when flutes were pulled out, and Jim hated the song more with each rendition.

A few bodies were carried from the chapel, but they could never tell if one of them was Will.

Mostly, they sat silent, tired, and cold in the wind and the rain and the fetid slop, and watched the soldados repair the presidio. When the sun peeked out, they warmed their backs.

"You're right, Noah," Ehrenberg said. "Being cold is preferable."

"Shut up," Noah replied.

"Didn't Dante say hell was a frozen place?" Daniel asked.

"You can shut up, too."

Jim pressed his icy nose into his knees.

Rumor had it that Fannin had left with Mexican Colonel Holzinger two days before to secure a ship for their passage out of Tejas. The thought cheered everyone but Jim. Being sent to some unknown land in the United States did not necessarily improve his situation, but he reminded himself it would be better to be free and far from here than dead. He could find his way home.

Toward mid-afternoon, nearly a hundred more prisoners arrived inside the ring. Some were Ward's men, the reinforcements the Texians had futilely hoped would appear on the horizon during the battle, but now captured just like the rest of them. Ehrenberg and the others greeted those they knew, while Noah opened his arms as if he were hosting a grand party. As for the rest, they had no feelings toward the scores of strangers from a militia captured on the coast in El Copano. If anything, they added to the competition for food.

Like everyone else, Jim made room and studied the newcomers.

"Would you look at her...." Ehrenberg said. He gave a low whistle, his sight trained beyond their company. Jim followed his eyes and saw two women walking beside the western wall with Mexican officers. At the vision of Eva, he froze.

"Which one?" Noah asked.

"The raven-haired fräulein, obviously."

Noah sucked his cheek. "She is a beauty. Wouldn't mind hugging her close. The other one's nice, too."

"Eh," Ehrenberg said.

Look at me, Jim thought. He stepped around his comrades and toed the invisible boundary.

The nearest guard narrowed his eyes, searched for what held his attention, and then glowered. "Canalla," he said, pushing at Jim with the butt of his musket.

Jim took a step back, but he only had eyes for Eva.

The soldier lost patience with him and lowered his bayonet, then moved to block Jim's vision.

Forced to focus on the soldado, Jim raised his hands. He took five paces back, trodding on the man sitting behind him. "Sorry," he mumbled down.

Eva entered a stone doorway and disappeared from sight.

Francisca needed only a single viewing to compel her to meet with Lieutenant Colonel Portilla about the treatment of the prisoners.

"I can do nothing more for them without direct orders from the General," he said. "It's not worth wasting our own food on them. General Urrea has written to the President recommending clemency, but…." Portilla shrugged.

"Fine. I understand, sir. But you will not prevent me from purchasing food from my own funds, will you?"

Portilla smirked. "If that is truly how you want to spend your money, my dear, I will not stand in your way."

Francisca straightened her shoulders and seemed to want to say more, but she didn't. "Thank you, sir," she said after a moment, and they left.

When they stepped back into the courtyard, Francisca covered her cheeks with her palms and stared at the sky above the fortress wall in thought. "We have time before dinner if we are quick. I don't want Telesforo to know."

The afternoon eroded alarmingly as they procured food from one provisioner's tent after another. Francisca paced and wrung her hands with each delay, and Eva watched the tortilla makers flip the flattened masa with steel fingers.

Unannounced, Kidisti appeared across the path, and Eva startled when she raised her eyes and noticed her watchful presence. At Eva's nod, her warden walked away. Her hands shook, betraying her flagging confidence, and she clasped them behind her back.

With the baskets finally full, Francisca looked at the setting sun and grasped the handles. She and Eva marched back to the prisoners with as much speed as the dignity of their positions allowed.

"Did you spend Telesforo's money or your own?" Eva asked.

Francisca, breathless from their pace, darted her eyes at her. "A little of both."

Tophe had their cash. Eva wondered if she should steal some or all of it. When they approached the parade ground, they slowed down. Soldiers lit torches around the perimeter.

"We need to hurry," Francisca whispered.

The prisoners noticed them and stood, clustering against the invisible barrier, while Francisca spoke to the guards. After searching the baskets, their sergeant gestured at several of his privates to form up around the ladies. The Texians shoved each other until one of their number shouted for his fellows to act like civilized men and line up in an orderly fashion.

As they received tortillas and a bit of dried beef, the prisoners thanked Francisca and Eva, kissing their hands. Eva spotted Jim next in line and almost dropped her basket, but managed to tear her eyes away. When he reached her, he cupped her hand in both of his and lifted it to his mouth. His eyes shone with tears. As she had at all the Texians, she smiled. His cheekbones jutted from his gaunt face, and she wanted to open a portal right here in front of everyone.

"You're very welcome, sir," she said in English and gently pulled her hand free. He took his tortilla and slid his eyes to Francisca. She placed beef in his hand, and he hazarded another glance at Eva. Eva kept her eyes on the next man.

Horror gripped her. Though Pump had told her Jim had joined a militia with Daniel Allen after being attacked in San Felipe, she had hoped her husband had ended up anywhere but here. Where was Pump now? Still searching for Jim? Her mind churned with the implications. Panic urged her to forget Francisca, but Eva brought herself under control. There was nothing she could do, not right then, and too many lives were on the line. Jim might be starving, but he was safe. For the moment.

Task complete, they hid their baskets in a storeroom and then slowed their walk toward Francisca's tent.

As Eva spent more time with Francisca, she marveled at the woman's compassion, now that it was real to her. A question grew inside her until she couldn't contain it. "Why do you want to help these men who meant to rebel and steal Tejas for themselves? You seem to be the only one who cares."

Her words caused Francisca to freeze in her tracks and peer back at her in confusion. "Why would you not? They're humans, just like we are, with mothers and sisters who love them. Wives and children, maybe. How much more reason do we need? I would not want my brother to be treated as such. Or

Telesforo. It shames me our government would stoop to such behavior. To pretend we do not have to follow the rules of war."

"I'm amazed you have the courage to stand up to the soldiers, the officers even. All alone." Eva caught a glimpse of her own programming, hardwired from pre-adolescence to obey authority.

Francisca tipped her head, and her lips parted in an evaluating smile. "I can't imagine standing by and saying nothing."

Ashamed, Eva stared at her friend's feet. Before her stood a brave woman who saw the world simply and clearly, and she envied her. To hide the storm in her heart, she said instead, "There's a man among the prisoners I want to get released."

Francisca lifted a brow and resumed their path. "Oh? You'll have to point him out to me," she said. "Does he have any skills? Doctor? Craftsman?"

Eva shook her head. "No, none of those things. But he is a dear friend from childhood. I can only imagine he is here because he has been forced."

Seemingly deep in thought, Francisca's gaze focused on the ground passing beneath her feet. "There may be something I can do. I will think on it. How is his Spanish?"

Eva wagged her head. "A little… sparse."

"Typical Anglo. They see no need to learn the language of their adoptive country."

When they reached the tent, Telesforo didn't question where they had been, and they left immediately to return to the fort.

Though comfortable inside the stone walls, dinner with the officers was a chilly affair for Eva, sitting across from Tophe. Francisca and Colonel Garay discussed *Sancho Saldaña o El castellano de Cuéllar,* which they had both read. Garay felt José de Espronceda took his romantic notions too far, but he listened attentively to Francisca's defense.

Telesforo's eyes gleamed with pride in his wife's intellect.

Lieutenant Colonel Portilla, on the other hand, squinted, lost, and unable to follow the conversation.

Tophe ate with single-minded purpose, immune to the disapproving looks his peers cast his way. When her partner lifted his gaze to meet her eye, a cold stranger glared back at her, and she imagined a target forming on her throat. If he was asked a direct question, he answered, but French vowels tainted his Spanish. He left at the conclusion of the meal without a word, and Garay pursed his lips.

As they passed the prisoners on their way back, Eva surveyed her options. She didn't see any. Completely exposed, torches illuminated the parade ground, and dozens of infantrymen surrounded the milling herd of prisoners.

"Do you see the man who looks like an Indian?" she said into Francisca's ear. They walked arm in arm beside her husband.

Francisca peeked over her shoulder. "Yes."

"What are you two whispering about?" Telesforo asked.

Francisca laughed. "Ladies' complaints, my heart. Would you like me to say more?"

Telesforo grunted with good humor. “No, thank you. I believe I can continue to live in ignorance.”

Chapter 20

Eva

Jim's expectant face followed Eva every time she appeared. When they fed the prisoners in the morning, his eyes questioned. By the evening, he looked confused. She silently cursed him for being unable to read a note she could have passed him. With no other option, she squeezed his hand under the tortilla to reassure him, but he pulled away.

Throughout the day, Francisca spoke to every prisoner she could, including the doctors and the wounded, though it was hard to converse with many of the able-bodied men and boys. Francisca questioned them in Spanish but switched to English at their blank, slack-jawed faces. In answer to queries, they told her where they were from and their occupations back in the States.

Jim hung back, and Eva willed him to step nearer, to try to talk to them. She widened her eyes at him, but he gave her his back.

The rumors amongst the officers and enlisted men put Francisca on alert. During the evening meal, the guards questioned the wisdom of feeding the prisoners, and Francisca watched for messengers arriving.

That night in Francisca's tent, Eva tried to sleep, but her mind churned. As soon as Telesforo began to snore, Francisca rose, and Eva joined her.

Eva thought of Jim as she fastened her snakeskin belt around her waist and stuck the pistol through it. Her quiver and bow case stood against Francisca's cot. After a moment of indecision, she laced her arm through the shoulder strap. Telesforo snorted in his sleep and rolled over, causing the women to freeze in place. After several watchful moments, Eva followed Francisca out of the tent and to the fortress.

Inside the presidio, the soldiers manned their posts. The shadows pooled in inky, empty spaces where the torches didn't reach. Francisca's brow creased, and she extended her stride. They headed straight for the candlelit doorway, knowing they would find the officers there.

"Such cruel, contradictory instructions!" Portilla was saying as they entered. He stood next to Colonel Garay, who sat with his head in his hands, and the men acknowledged the ladies with a single distracted glance.

Francisca picked up the two letters from Garay's desk.

Outraged at her brazen behavior, Portilla opened his mouth and looked at his superior officer. Garay just watched her, dejected.

Eva read over her shoulder.

March 23, 1836

Officer Commanding the Post of Goliad,

I order that you should give immediate effect to the Tornel Decree in respect to all those foreigners. I trust that, in reply to this, you will inform me that public vengeance has been satisfied by the punishment of such detestable delinquents.

Antonio López de Santa Anna
President of the United Mexican States

Beneath his signature, a seal had pressed an upright arm and dagger with the legend "Mano y Clavo" into a circle of black wax. Francisca shuffled the first letter behind the second.

March 26, 1836

Lieutenant Colonel Portilla,

I order that you put the prisoners to work repairing the town and the presidio. Treat them with every respect afforded to prisoners of war, including regular rations. Colonel Fannin, in particular, is to be treated with all the respect due to an officer of his rank.

José Cosme de Urrea y Elías González
General, Army of the United Mexican States

"When did these arrive?" Francisca asked.

"Within hours of each other," Portilla responded.

"What are your intentions?" Francisca asked Garay.

Portilla took the letters from her hands. "To obey the President's instructions to the letter." He folded the orders and tucked them into his coat. "It won't be easy," he said, focusing on Garay. "How do we accomplish it? How many of our soldiers will be unwilling to carry out their duty? I'll need to double the guard, so at least one of the two shoots!"

Garay straightened from his slumped position.

"Please delay," Francisca said. "Much can be done in a few days. I have friends near the President whom he can't afford to disoblige. A rider could start for Bexar tonight with a letter from you."

Portilla frowned. "Madam Alavez, I would not write that letter for all the gold in Mexico."

"At least spare Miller's men. The ones from the boat captured on the coast. They never raised arms against us."

Portilla looked at Garay, and his colonel shrugged. "They're a gray area," Garay said.

"I'll make white armbands to set them apart," Francisca said.

Garay drummed his fingers on the desk. "Yes, fine. Do as she wishes regarding Miller's men."

Portilla saluted. "If I may be excused, Colonel, there is much I need to prepare."

Garay waved him away, then gazed up at Francisca and Eva, twirling his quill, a pained expression on his face.

"Sir, quite a few of the rebels would be valuable servants for the duration of the war," Francisca said. "There are several tradesmen, not to mention the two doctors."

Garay lifted a brow. "What are you suggesting?"

"A note from you to the guards will allow me to remove them."

"The doctors and those wounded should remain where they are, but I can let you remove the useful prisoners from the parade ground. Give me their names."

Francisca recited the short list as she peered down at the scrap of paper he wrote upon. At Eva's intake of breath, Francisca gave a brief shake of her head.

"Bring me the white armbands, and I will see they are distributed," Garay said, handing her the message for the guards.

"Thank you, sir."

When they were outside, Eva said, "I wanted to add my friend's name to the list."

"We will make an extra armband for him. Those men will likely be released sooner, and he'll be safe from the front lines."

Eva couldn't fault her reasoning, but an uneasiness settled in her stomach, and she flexed her jaw to unclench her teeth.

At the circle of prisoners, Jim stood up when he saw her. Francisca handed the guard the note, and he read out the names of those deemed worth keeping alive.

"You are to go with these ladies," he said. The selected Texians shuffled nervously and hugged their elbows. Francisca did nothing to reassure them.

Jim stared down at Eva, the invisible bars between them. The betrayal on his face cut her. She pleaded with her eyes, but he stepped back when a soldier approached to drive him off.

At the door of the chapel, Father Molloy greeted the group. Francisca whispered in his ear, and he led the way to the vestry. "I can keep them in here."

Francisca handed him the message from Garay. "To be safe, I will acquire a note for the doctors and their assistants and bring it to you," she said. "Otherwise, they may get caught up when our soldiers come for their patients."

The priest covered his mouth as he realized the full horror of what she was saying. None of the wounded prisoners understood what was being said around them. If they knew, Eva wondered, what would they do? What *could* they do?

The women stayed in the vestry and removed their white petticoats. Eva enlisted the prisoners they had rescued to help tear the cloth into strips.

"What's goin' on, ma'am?" one of them asked.

Eva didn't know what to say.

"You are useful to the Mexican army," Francisca said in English. "You will receive orders tomorrow as to your duties. Until then, you will remain here. Do not leave this room."

The prisoners cut their eyes to each other. The one who had spoken brought the petticoat to his teeth and pulled the fabric apart. When they had counted out seventy-six armbands, Francisca gathered them up, and they returned to Garay. At her persistence, he wrote a second note for the doctors, and while he had his quill out, he wrote a message to the guards about the armbands.

"Miller's men and the Indian," Francisca repeated. Eva opened her mouth to have him write Jim's name instead but then thought better of it.

"Yes, yes," Garay said. "I will send these over."

"And…" Eva said, "Daniel Allen. Please, add Daniel Allen to the list."

"I am willing to include the Indian, who is here against his will, but you are asking for a second man? Taken during battle?"

Eva swallowed. "I believe he is actually loyal to Mexico."

Garay tapped his quill.

"I myself heard him speak out against the rebels," Eva said.

Garay bent his head over the paper. His quill hovered, but then he shook his head. With a grimace, he looked up at them, shook his head again, and scrawled out DANIEL ALLEN.

Eva let the breath out she had been holding, took one of the armbands, and split it down its length. "Seventy-seven."

Garay darted his eyes to heaven and closed them.

Francisca and Eva thanked him.

"What else can we do?" Francisca asked as they left. "There are so many!"

Eva took her hand. They headed out of the fort, passing the sea of prisoners on the parade ground, but she paused. "I want to wait and make sure my friend gets his armband."

"I need to keep moving," Francisca said. "I can't stand still. I need to think."

Eva reviewed the steps they had taken. Almost all the lives Francisca would save at Goliad had been arranged. She hadn't seen any sign of Tophe, but other men would need her in the coming days, and tomorrow held last-minute rescues. Indecision pulled her in opposite directions, but the bond tying her to Jim tightened, making her choice for her.

"All right," Eva said, letting her go.

As she watched Francisca walk away, Eva picked at a cuticle and nearly sprinted after her before refocusing on her husband.

From within the guarded circle, Jim stared at her with his arms crossed over his chest and no expression on his face. With a disgusted glare, he turned away just as she brought her hand up to cuff her upper arm, pantomiming the white ribbon. Did he see? She didn't think he saw. Stubborn, sulky man, she thought. She waited for him to look her way again.

A pistol jabbed her in her ribs.

"It's me this time," Tophe said. "Let's go home."

Too angry to look at her, Jim returned to Daniel, lying down with his back against his friend's. The rest of the prisoners slept. Spirits had been high the day before because Fannin had returned with the Mexican Colonel Holzinger, so surely that meant a ship had been arranged, but Jim read the body language of the guards. A strange mood had descended on the entire presidio.

He seethed at the thought of Eva. It was like Mission Concepción all over again, minus the chains and daily mass. At least there, he had been fed. They should be home by now, eating Ohayaa's and Tʉe Tseenaʔ's cooking. She could have even gotten Daniel and Will to safety, too. At the thought of his brother's wives, he tasted honey, and slow-roasted meat melted on his tongue. Fat ran down his chin. When he wiped his mouth, he was surprised his hand didn't come away greasy. Jim tried to remember why they had ended up here, but cobwebs trapped his thoughts. How long was she going to let him sit captive?

Though still dark, the fortress woke early. Jim sat up, and Daniel did the same, scratching his beard. Jim hadn't told Daniel about Eva because he hadn't figured out yet how to explain her presence at the fort, and they had never met. Now, it seemed, he didn't need to bother.

"Miller!" one of the guards called. The Nashville Battalion, those who had been captured at the coast, kept themselves separate from the Goliad soldiers. The unblooded boys claimed to have been mistreated in Copano after their ship had been taken. None of the veterans of the days and nights in the chapel wanted to hear about it.

Daniel nudged him. The newcomers were putting on white armbands. "Wonder what that's for?"

One of Miller's men strode toward them with strips of cloth in his hand. He studied Jim but shifted his gaze to address Daniel. "Do you know a Daniel Allen?"

The big man pushed to his feet. "Yes, that's me."

Miller's man handed him the ribbons. "We assumed he's the Indian," he said, gesturing down at Jim. "There's one for him, too."

"What are these for?" Daniel asked.

Jim hauled himself up and glanced around. None of the other Goliad soldiers had received armbands.

The man lifted a shoulder. "Special work detail, I think." He tilted his head at Jim. "You don't look Indian to me. You look like a muddy white man in Indian clothing."

"You're right. I'm not. My people have never called themselves Indians."

The man scowled. "You know what I mean." He walked back to his side of the yard.

Daniel pondered the cloth in his hands. "I don't know about this. How did the officer know my real name?" He handed Jim one of the strips but placed the other in his pocket.

"I think we should put them on," Jim said. Eva's smiling face crisped in his mind, and he begged her forgiveness. "Here, help me with mine."

Daniel gritted his teeth.

"Really," Jim said. "I think it's important we're wearing these."

Daniel sighed and tied Jim's. Jim opened his palm for Daniel's, and the man dragged it from his pocket. He shook his head, then peeked down at his arm.

"Don't take that off," Jim said, jabbing his finger into Daniel's chest. "For anything."

A moment later, he noticed Miller's men studying him, so he lowered his eyes and turned his back. Daniel's brow furrowed over his shoulder, and Jim heard footsteps trudging in their direction. Left with no other choice, he took a deep breath and faced them.

Eight men glowered at him.

"We don't have any backstabbing, murderous Indians in our battalion. I'll be damned if we start with you. Take off that ribbon," one of them said.

Jim crossed his arms. "No."

"Do, or we'll take it off for you."

"You're welcome to try."

The man's fists clenched, and he swung. Jim dodged the blow, and Daniel stepped between them, throwing his own punch. Three other men attacked Jim at once. His hands and feet flew until a direct hit forced the air from his lungs, and they tackled him.

Musket shots cracked, and soldados shoved bayonets in their faces. Before someone removed the last attacker, Jim landed a final punch. Daniel pulled him to his feet, and Noah and Ehrenberg stood beside him, their faces bloodied.

When Jim checked his arm, the band was gone.

Chapter 21

Eva

"Take my arm," Tophe said, tucking Eva's pistol and knife into his belt. He kept his own in her ribs as they exited the presidio and marched east toward a stand of trees. Frogs peeped, making the world sound wet.

"I can't go back home," Eva said.

Tophe didn't answer.

To match his stride, she lengthened hers. "Can you please put the pistol away, and we talk?"

When he still didn't respond, she halted and took it from his unresistant hand, her own firearm remaining in his belt. "I'm not going home. I can't. For one thing, my belly is going to give me away in a matter of weeks. A couple of months, tops."

"There's a fix for that."

She resisted the urge to take a bead on his chest. "Not in Axis Mundi."

"Outside of Axis Mundi, clearly," he said. "We get you home, and then we ask for leave immediately."

"We just abandon the mission here? You know that's not an option."

"We're one of their best teams. We haven't failed in a long time, and the council will understand, considering the T'ibek'a. I think they'll grant us leave for that very reason." Tophe pointed at her temple. "And you have an injury to recover from. None of that will be a lie."

He sounded so reasonable. His words turned the knob, opening a door to Lux Libera, and light glimmered from a comfortable, secure, familiar beyond. "You've put a lot of thought into this," Eva said.

"It's all I've been thinking about since you left me in El Copano. I gave up on our mission that night." When she lifted a brow, he added, "Well, maybe not that night, but definitely since we arrived here in Goliad."

"Tophe," she said. "I can't go back with you. I'm *not* going back with you."

He glanced over her head at the trees. A golden ribbon lined the horizon beneath the heavy clouds, and the first ray of dawn brightened his face. She could see him thinking, and every muscle in her body tensed. Without further warning, he ran toward her and caught her over his shoulder.

Adrenaline lent her strength and speed, and Eva formed a portal. She tuned Tophe's strings along with her own in a breathtaking snap, returning them to their original spot.

He didn't break stride, and she jumped them again five times.

"I can do that all day," she said when he set her down on her feet. She forced herself to breathe normally. If he hadn't stopped, she couldn't have managed another one without resting. Her empty stomach threatened to dry heave in protest.

Winded, he paced in front of her. He jabbed in the direction of the trees with his finger and then dropped his hands onto his knees. As he straightened, his face contorted, and he took her pistol out of his belt. "I can't lie to the Elders, and I'm not letting you stay here to be caught by Lux Libera. I won't lose you like that."

Eva scoffed. "You're not going to shoot me. Put that down."

"I'd rather see you in the next life than know I'll never see you again at all."

Eva's palms broke into a sweat. She jerked up the pistol she had taken from him and trained it on his forehead. "We don't know that life works that way, Tophe. It's just a guess."

"It makes the most sense to me," he said, cocking the flint.

Alarmed, she tossed her pistol into the grass. "Look, Tophe. Look. Look at us." She showed him her empty palms. "This is crazy. I'm not going to shoot you. You're not going to shoot me."

He pulled the trigger. The pistol smoked after a loud crack, and they stared at each other in shock. Eva looked down at herself, patting her chest. While she checked for wounds, he ran toward her. She opened her hands to make a portal, but he took her to the ground. Sitting on her hips, he wrapped his hands around her neck and burrowed his thumbs into her throat. Tears poured down his face and dripped onto hers.

"I'm sorry, Eva. I'm sorry," he said in an unending stream.

She bucked beneath him, hunting for his foot with her own. Her bow case and quiver dug into her back. She found his ankle and brought her other foot up behind her hip, but her vision dimmed, and her heel couldn't find purchase. Panicked, she pulled back on his pinkies, and he released his grip.

Eva gasped for breath and pushed at his thighs, but he didn't move.

"I can't," Tophe said. "God help me, I can't." He leaned forward, his hands above either side of her head, closing his eyes against what he had tried to do.

She was pushing his chest when people ran into her periphery. Two knives flanked Tophe's neck.

"Get up," Kidisti said. "I'm surprised Mexican scouts aren't already over here. Seems like you would know better."

Tophe sat back on Eva's hips and raised his hands.

"You didn't tell us there were three of you," Ephrem said to Eva. To make Tophe stand, he pulled his elbow. Eva rolled to the side and cradled her neck. Tophe skidded blank eyes across her and his assailants, seemingly unsure where to focus.

When Eva could stand, she saw prisoners filing out of the fort. She noted the sun, and all thoughts flew out of her head as anxiety for her husband elbowed to the front of her mind. The sight kicked the breath from her lungs and refused to let them refill, and her tether to Jim jerked taut, pulling and demanding her immediate attention.

Kidisti held Tophe's arm. Eva rushed them, pushing Kidisti's knife arm across her chest and opening a portal. The three emerged in the middle of the prairie on the far horizon. In the blink of an eye, she jumped them again out of Ephrem's line of vision.

"How did you do that?" Kidisti asked, retreating several steps.

Eva grabbed her knife from Tophe's belt and turned on her. All she had to do was throw it. Seven months ago, she would have done so instantly, but now she hesitated.

Kidisti's eyes cut to the nearest tree several hundred yards away. "It's normal to have trouble surrendering your former partner," she said, her own knife pointed at Eva. "But this man needs to be brought to justice."

"What you're doing… it's wrong," Eva said. "I gave you my word. I said I will guard timelines, and I will, but not by throwing other travelers into the Abyss. I won't let you take him."

"It's the right thing to do."

"Is it?" Eva squinted her eyes. "You know…" she said, emphasizing with the point of her knife, "that's a universal trait between travelers and the Fated. We're all just humans justifying our choices to ourselves. We all think we're the good guys. It's heartbreaking!" A branching path snapped into existence. "You won't leave us in peace?"

"No, I am oath-bound." Kidisti squared her shoulders.

Eva flipped the knife to hold it by the blade, then swallowed, knowing she should plunge it into her own murderous breast. Kidisti's mouth rounded, and she pawed at her pistol.

Eva threw.

Kidisti studied her chest in shock, and her knees crumpled.

"We need to kill the other one," Tophe said.

While avoiding looking into the Guardian's stunned, blinking eyes, Eva yanked her knife out and drove it into Kidisti's neck, then opened a portal, returning them to their original fight.

Eva and Tophe peered into the trees, but the partner was gone. After a moment, Tophe walked several paces through the grass and retrieved Eva's pistol, still loaded. He handed it to her, eyes downcast.

Before she could find words, a great, rolling crescendo of musket fire echoed in the distance.

Chapter 22

Jim

"Take mine," Daniel said, fumbling at the knot under his arm. The fighters had dispersed.

"No," Jim said. "I told you. Do not take this off for anything."

Daniel continued to work at untying the fabric, but Jim took him by the arms and lowered his voice. "You have to trust me. I owe you a life. If I'm right, my debt to you is paid."

Daniel's face drained of color. "What about Will?"

"Think of Maggie and your children."

Daniel's hand sank, and the big man stared at Jim's chest.

"There is nothing you can do for Will. Nothing." Jim squeezed the big man's shoulders, giving them a little shake.

"I'd give him mine."

"No. He can't walk. We don't even know if he's still alive."

Daniel gnawed at his lower lip.

When his friend finally nodded, conceding their reality, Jim cupped the back of Daniel's neck. "You could just be sparing me from a work detail," Jim said, adding a shrug. "We'll just have to see."

Daniel smirked but was able to meet his eyes again.

Shouts from the guards roused the rest of the prisoners who had slept through the scuffle.

Spohn translated the command to gather their possessions and line up for a roll call.

"Did someone escape?" Noah asked. Their captors had never bothered with one since the ammunition wagon exploded.

Jim joined the Greys, and their line stretched toward the sally port. He answered to his name, and Daniel answered to his false one. Spohn reunited with them at the end of the line.

"What's going on?" Noah asked.

"I think we're being marched to Copano and then sailing to New Orleans," Spohn said, grinning.

Jim's spirits lifted, and the men around him hugged each other's necks. A Grey farther down the row leaned over and said, "The soldado down here said we're being formed to hunt cattle."

"On foot?" Noah asked. "That doesn't make any sense. They gonna let us borrow their horses?"

As Jim imagined them all riding straight for Nʉmʉnʉʉ Sookobitʉ on Mexican mounts, he chuckled. He was so ravenously drunk on hunger he couldn't stop, laughing so hard his sides hurt. Daniel knit his brow at Jim's behavior.

"You know what I think?" Ehrenberg said. "I think they're marching us to Matamoros and prison… or worse, to be chained slaves deep in the Mexican mines."

"Nah," another man said. "Remember what Holzinger said? 'Eight days, then home and liberty.' Today's the eighth day."

At his reminder, the paranoia dissipated down the line.

Ready to move and escape these walls, Jim shuffled his bare, muddy feet in place. He didn't care that they would be bloody by the end of the trail.

"Nashville Battalion," the Mexican officer called. "Bandas blancas," he said, pointing at his own upper arm.

"That's you," Jim said to Daniel.

"Perhaps I did end up on a work detail, and you're headed home." Daniel's smile didn't reach his eyes.

Jim took his hand. "If I find out that's the case, I will return." The ground shifted under his feet as he second-guessed Eva's involvement, and he debated swapping places. "The fact they knew your real name has to mean something."

More confident, Daniel returned his handshake and joined Miller's men. After they assembled, the sailors captured on the coast marched out of the southern wall sally port and turned left.

Then, it was the Goliad soldiers' turn. The guards organized them into double lines and gave the order to march. They passed through the gate, and Jim took a deep breath, smelling fresh spring grass. If he thought he could have gotten very far, he would have run.

A cluster of women lined the path, and he looked for Eva but didn't see her. Their faces ranged from pure hatred to indifference to pity.

"Spohn!" a soldado called from the gate. Spohn, who marched behind him, hopped out of line to hurry back.

A portion of cavalry waited for them in three formations of triple-sided hollow squares. The Greys were herded into the first, then sealed with another line of cavalrymen.

The Mexicans wore their dress uniforms. Crisscrossed white sashes gleamed over their blue coats, so clean. In contrast, Jim could feel vermin crawling over his skin and resisted the urge to scratch his scalp.

"What about the wounded?" Noah asked. "What about Pettus?"

His questions brought Will to Jim's mind, but no one responded because no one knew the answer.

When all militias were contained in separate, secure groups, the Greys were led east down the slope, and their cavalry escort spread out along the prairie. Four lines of infantrymen waited for them on the road, and the prisoners' column slid into the middle.

"Takes two soldados to control one Texian," Noah observed. Heads rose, and shoulders straightened.

"Plus, cavalry," Ehrenberg said.

After so many chilly nights, the muggy spring air laid heavy dew on the grass. Jim measured his thighs with his hands. They had melted away over the past week, and his lungs labored to keep pace, which surprised and irritated him. Thirsty, he cast his eyes toward the belt of the soldado marching next to Ehrenberg. He turned to the soldado beside himself and the one behind him. None of the soldados carried water gourds. Or bedrolls. Or knapsacks with rations.

The Greys traveled northeast toward the San Antonio River and Victoria. Jim craned his neck to check behind their column, but the other two groups of Goliad prisoners had not followed them. Unnerved and confused, he faced the front.

"Why are we headed the wrong way? Copano is in the opposite direction," Noah whispered.

"The port at Velasco is this way. Quintana, too," Ehrenberg said. "Maybe that's where we're going."

Noah relaxed. "Makes sense," he said. "They're closer to the United States, anyway."

Jim decided starvation made him imagine things. He must have misunderstood Pump and Eva. If the Mexicans had intended to kill them, they would have done so long ago. And why would they have told them to bring their belongings? Those thoughts pricked his conscience. What if the armband designated who was to die? Had he sent Daniel to his death?

His own deafening will to survive drowned out his sudden uncertainty and guilt. He had made the right decision at the time. If he chose wrong, there was nothing he could do about it now. Unsoothed by his selfish argument, Jim grimaced. No, he told himself. It must have been Eva, and he chose correctly. Daniel was safe. Maybe they were all safe.

In front of him, Ehrenberg glanced over his shoulder every ten paces. Jim retreated into his own numb thoughts. Too exhausted to speak anymore, the Greys as a whole fell silent, but the usually talkative Mexican soldiers had yet to utter a word.

Jim listened to the trudging of more than three hundred feet and ignored the stones that cut his bare soles. He pondered the profile of the soldado marching beside him. The man was aware of his attention but kept his eyes straight ahead. Ehrenberg dropped his knapsack in the grass, and Jim watched as it drifted by like a stick down a stream.

Ahead, the San Antonio River came into view. His dry mouth cracked open, and he could taste the water on his tongue. When the Mexican officer veered them to the left and off the road, Jim's one-track mind screamed in annoyance.

As they reached a mesquite brush fence, the soldados on the right beside Jim and Ehrenberg stopped marching and held back. Without hesitation, the flanking soldados joined their comrades to form a double line three steps to the left of the prisoners' column. The fresh cut ends of the branches shone white, and Jim thought of catching his stallion, of Eva, of bullets. He hid his mind from her.

The officer called a halt. Once in place, the soldados stared at the ground, while the cavalry scattered across the grassland.

"Arrodillarse!"

Jim sniffed. He used that command on captives. In confusion, the Texians darted their eyes at each other. None of the others complied because none of them understood the order, and Jim wasn't about to kneel to anyone.

Between the soldados and the prisoners, the officer strode down the line. "¿Quien habla español?"

No one answered. Close to the end of the line, Jim peered behind himself at the thorns. Beyond, the cavalrymen rested their lances across their horses' shoulders, and mist swirled in the hollows.

From the southwest, they heard a faint cry of, "Liberty! Texas!" and then an enormous volley crackled through the distant trees toward them.

The front row of soldados dropped to one knee.

"Oh, God," Noah said.

"Listen to that shooting! They're killing the other militias!" someone cried. "Wake up!"

A man fell to his knees and prayed aloud for forgiveness from his god.

"Mercy!"

Many in the line pleaded with their executioners.

"Shut up!" someone shouted. "If we are to die, let us die like brave men!"

The officer drew his sword, his face twisting. In the distance, they heard faint staccatos of agony.

"Arrodillarse!" the Mexican captain repeated.

Again, no one moved. When he raised his sword, the soldados placed their muskets on their hips. A second wave of musket fire, followed by louder, closer screams, rippled from the west.

The fear haze in Jim's starved mind cleared, replaced by crystalline rage. He would take at least one enemy with him. With an explosive burst of strength, he lowered his head and pushed off with his feet.

The pans flashed.

Chapter 23

Eva

"Find the partner. Meet back here," Eva said, forming a portal. "My husband is among the prisoners."

Tophe opened his mouth to speak but then ran to the trees without responding.

Eva materialized outside Garay's tent. She sprinted through the orchard, scanning Miller's men.

Like horror-struck statues, they gaped at the slaughter beyond the trees. Silent tears streamed down their faces, each man disbelieving what they were seeing. Utterly devoid of humor, others leaked terrorized, red-faced laughter through clenched teeth, their swearing laced with demonic, impotent passion.

In the street, Francisca stood larger than life, her hair blowing around her. She screamed and cursed Portilla, the other officers, and the enlisted men. Within the gated walls, soldados carried the wounded to the parade ground, where privates pointed muskets at the men lying on pallets and fired.

Jim wasn't there among the white-armbanded men. She strangled her panic and jumped to the southwest firing line, where she knew the Red Rovers and Westover's Regulars had been taken. Through the smoke, soldados stabbed survivors with bayonets. Ragged Texians stumbled through the grass toward the trees. Cavalrymen blocked their paths.

Eva jumped down the line in a blur, but the bodies lay jumbled, one on top of another.

Pump appeared, frantically searching the field. He startled when he saw her, and they drew the attention of the nearest infantrymen.

Within seconds, she jumped them to safety. "Do a more thorough check here," she said, swallowing a dozen questions. Pump nodded, and she opened a portal to the northwest.

When Eva arrived at the second firing line, the officer there was grabbing a prisoner by the shoulder, forcing him to face a brush pile. These were the Georgia Battalion and Kentucky Mustangs. The other volunteers complied, begging to be spared, as they rotated in place. Eva's sight skipped ahead of her comprehension, and she forced herself to slow down. When she was sure she hadn't overlooked Jim, she faced the east. The officer raised his sword, and a deafening percussion echoed in her ears.

She missed her target, landing south of where the Greys were to be executed. In a blink, she corrected her position, and when she appeared in the right place, the soldados were lowering their muskets.

Her heart soared at the sight of Jim, so close to the end of the line. The next instant, he tucked into a run toward the firing line, oblivious to her, his features battle-fierce, and she jumped, aiming for his trajectory. The ear-splitting crack of musket fire met

Eva just as Jim ran into her chest. She created a new portal behind them, simultaneously looping an arm around his back, and they fell together.

Jim landed on top of her and pushed up in confusion. On the ground beside them, Eva formed a portal one-handed and rolled them into it. After the fourth compulsive, fear-driven jump, Jim grabbed her wrists, wrapped his arms around her, and wept. She tried to lift her right arm, but it was too heavy. As she covered his face in kisses, their tears mingled, and beneath her exploratory fingers, his ribs jutted like blades.

When he squeezed tighter, she cried out as if someone had taken an ax to her shoulder. Jim helped her sit up, and as she gazed, exhausted, at his chest, she noticed a bloody hole in his shirt. He inspected her clavicle and then stood to examine it from behind.

"I think the ball went through clean, but your collarbone is broken, notsaʔka," he said, kneeling before her.

Barely listening, she reached toward him and raised his shirt, while he glanced down, surprised. She helped him remove it with a shaky hand, her right arm useless in her lap. A pulpy bruise spread from the middle of his left breast. Eva gingerly pressed the skin around it and plucked the ball with her fingers. The skin around Jim's eyes tightened, but he didn't cry out. Fresh blood flowed down his chest. Within moments, it ceased like a dam emptied.

Eva released a similar emptying breath and held it up before him with a mirthless laugh.

When he took it from her, he wiped the blood off, head shaking.

Despite her shoulder screaming, Eva lowered herself onto her side. She would have toppled otherwise. Every cell in her body seized and refused to produce another ounce of energy.

Jim's eyebrows scrunched, and he stroked the hair from her face.

"I'm okay," she said. "I just need to rest, but only for a moment. We don't have time. We need to get back to Pump and Tophe. There's an enemy traveler we need to kill. Someone like me. We'll never be safe if he gets away."

Jim lay beside her and placed a hand over the baby, then stood up as if reminded of something he had forgotten. "I'll be right back," he said, staggering away.

Water bubbled over nearby rocks, and she compelled herself to follow him but stopped after the third step. The ends of her broken bone ground together.

At her cry of pain, Jim returned, wiping his mouth.

"We need to go," Eva said. Her words came out in gasps.

He pressed his lips together and tilted his head as if to protest.

"This can't wait, Jim. This absolutely cannot wait." She lifted her arm.

Reluctantly, he took her waist, and they stepped into the portal.

Chapter 24

Jim

When Eva hunched over and vomited, Jim hopped back. They were concealed by a thicket of undergrowth behind the firing line. The smell of gunpowder hung in the air, and smoke drifted toward them, while hazy figures plundered the bodies of his comrades. Jim worried the executioners might have heard her.

"I don't think I can jump again," Eva whispered. "I don't know what's wrong with me. I didn't feel this way when I traveled from the village to Pump's farm. I should have been able to jump us farther."

"Could it be the baby or… and I'm just guessing here… the *hole* in your shoulder?" Jim raised an eyebrow.

"Mmm, could be that."

After he helped her remove her bow case to lie down, he discovered entrance and exit holes in the quiver. Peering down the tube, he inspected the shattered ends of two shafts. Their fletching had been sheared off by the ball meant for him, but the rest of the arrows had survived unscathed.

"Pump was here. Checking for you," she said, interrupting his astonishment. "Take my knife and pistol."

"No."

"I have my others." Eva lifted an ankle to show a hidden sheath strapped to her calf. "Besides, this is my throwing arm. I won't be able to do anything with it."

"I'm leaving you the pistol." Jim untied her knife belt, wrapped it around his waist, then strung the bow and bent down to kiss Eva's forehead. Under his gentle lips, her eyes remained closed, and he caressed her cheek. With her good hand, she pressed the tips of his fingers to her face and smiled.

With a last backward glance, he crept through the brush. The cavalrymen had followed the escaping prisoners and were no longer in sight. Though several infantrymen still rummaged through pockets and removed clothing, with the butchering done, many had joined the foot chase. One body gasped as a soldado unknotted its silk neckerchief. The private shrieked in fright, and Jim watched as he ensured it returned to being just a corpse. When the private was satisfied, he stripped it.

"Jim!"

Jim turned at the sharp whisper and nearly fell over. "I'm supposed to be looking for *you*."

Pump lifted from his knees and embraced him. "Which militia were you with?"

"The Greys." Disoriented after jumping, Jim searched for the sun and then took his bearings. "I think we were northeast of here. We were taken northeast of the presidio, at least. I didn't see where the other militias went, but they didn't follow us."

Pump widened his eyes and whistled. "And Eva found you in time." He squeezed Jim's arms and ran his hands over him, then examined the bloody hole in his shirt.

"Just a bruise," Jim said.

"Good. Your face is a mess, but otherwise, you don't seem too much the worse for wear. Nothing a few meals won't fix." Pump shook his head. "I was just about to leave to search the other sites and hopefully find Eva when I happened to see you from behind." He sat back on his heels. "Where is she?"

Jim pointed to the spot he had left her, and Pump jumped them there.

At the sight of her, Pump's joy hardened to concern. She didn't open her eyes, even when he touched her cheek.

Jim's own anxiety spiked. He peeked back over his shoulder through the brush. Plenty of Mexicans could overhear any noise they made. While he patted her other cheek, he whispered, "Eva…."

She mumbled to herself and frowned.

"How much did she jump?" Pump asked.

"Four times after she found me. Plus, a fifth here."

"There's no telling how many before I saw her. She just needs rest. And a doctor, by the look of that shoulder." Pump picked her up. "Grab on to me," he said to Jim.

Jim rose and grasped a fistful of Pump's coat. The soldados, still plundering, noticed their movement. Bloodied bayonets ran toward them, but in the next instant, the enemies were replaced by empty trees and smoke on the horizon three miles away.

As Pump set her down, Eva roused. "Pump," she said, eyes half-lidded. "Thank God." She hissed when he tried to lower her onto her back and stayed seated upright instead. "Where have you been?"

"Everywhere, feels like. Went to Goliad first, but the Texians were already in the chapel. I checked the wounded and even dug up the graves after the field cleared." He cast a glance in Jim's direction. "No Jim there." The corners of his mouth lifted without humor.

A cold shadow passed through Jim's soul.

"Next, I went to Victoria and then Sam Houston's men on the march."

"How did you know to look for me?" Jim asked.

Eva put her hand on his arm. "There's no time for that." She turned back to Pump. "We need to help Tophe."

"Help Tophe?" By the scowl on Pump's face, she might as well have asked him to jump into a cesspit. The older man stroked the top of his head.

"Have you heard of the T'ibek'a?" Eva asked.

Comprehension dawned. "I haven't heard of them in particular, but I was just getting to that. A member of a guardian sect intercepted me when I was searching through Houston's lines. He seemed to know what I looked like."

"Yes, they tagged us the moment we rode into El Copano. They assumed you were my partner. I thought he would have a harder time finding you."

"You know, I never could shake the feeling we were being followed while I was in camp there." Pump showed them the back of his head. "He knocked me out once, but I came to before he could haul me back to his home line. Led him on a merry chase, but he kept finding me."

"The Guardian was supposed to be letting me recruit you. He lied to me." Her face darkened. "They put a beacon in my arm." Eva displayed the wound near her elbow.

Pump's eyes rounded.

Jim's emotions swam close to the surface, bewilderment and impatience, no longer containable. "I need to know what's going on!"

At his outburst, Eva and Pump shut their mouths and focused on him.

"I'm sorry," Eva said. She shielded her eyes, glancing at the sun and biting her lip.

To bring him up to speed, Pump spoke for her until Eva took over.

For the first time, Jim noticed the bruises around her neck. All doubts were gone after that. "I'm with Pump. We're not helping him. We're going to kill them both."

"Did you not hear what I said?" Eva asked. "Tophe stopped. He could have killed me, but he didn't."

The heat building in Jim's chest propelled him to stand, and he gazed down at her upturned face. "Did he change his mind, or did he just lose courage for a moment?"

"He changed his mind."

Her words curdled his stomach. Blind trust in an untrustworthy man. That's all Jim saw and had no answer for.

When he didn't respond, she unclenched the fist twisting her skirt, revealing damp wrinkles. "We're wasting time."

At his glance to Pump, the older man stared up at him and nodded.

"You agree with me or her?" Jim asked.

"You," Pump said.

Eva's knees bounced. "What's the compromise here?" she asked, turning in the direction she wanted to head.

"Is your injury keeping you here or your promise to me?" Jim asked.

Her head swiveled back. "My promise to you, of course." Her eyes flashed, and she staggered to her feet, hiding a grimace. "I told you; I only needed a moment to rest."

Pump shifted in his seat and trained a tense gaze on the horizon.

Eva held her elbow. "What are we doing?" she asked, eyes darting between them. "I'm the only one who knows Tophe. I need you both to trust me when I say I trust him. I can't leave him to a Guardian who wants to throw him into the Abyss."

When Jim jerked his head toward the open prairie and paced away, Eva fell in step beside him. He stopped out of earshot of Pump.

"Why did you leave me to sit a captive, Eva?"

She inhaled sharply, and tears sprang to her eyes. He forced himself not to look away.

"I didn't intend to leave you that way. There was no way to get to you without anyone seeing me."

"And this Angel of Goliad? She was more important than exposing yourself to rescue me, your husband? And now Tophe, too?"

As if he had slapped her in the face, her cheeks reddened.

"Let's go home," he said. "I think the compromise is we disappear and let them both live."

"What happened to your white armband? Did they not give it to you?"

"No, they gave it to me. Then they took it away again because they didn't want an Indian in the Nashville Battalion." A bitterness Kuhtu would recognize settled in his heart.

Eva flinched and shut her eyes. "And Daniel Allen?" she asked without opening them.

"Safe. Thank you." Thinking of his friend, he softened toward her. "He was the only one worth saving this Angel over me for."

"All of Miller's men were against you?"

"Enough."

"But not all." Eva seemed to hang onto an answer she hoped he would give.

"I don't know. The rest stood by while it happened."

"Maybe they didn't know what was happening."

The earnestness in her voice confused him. "Maybe." What answer was she hoping for?

Her frown deepened.

"What?" Jim asked.

"I don't know. I guess I want them to be worthy of saving. Even though I just told Tophe that one action — or inaction in this case — shouldn't decide the worth of an entire lifetime of choices." She massaged her forehead.

Jim shrugged, irritation mounting. "I don't know them. They can only be enemies to me now."

Eva sighed. "And you don't know Tophe either. I know his heart. Please don't make me choose between you and him. This one choice does not define my love for you. It's just unfinished business. I have to see this through, and then I will be free. Any future missions I undertake will be by our mutual decision. Preferably with you by my side."

Jim reached out and cupped a hand around the back of her neck. He grazed the circling bruise with his thumb, and she tilted her head away, wincing.

"Tophe thought he was saving me from existing in eternal darkness, unable to be reborn. He did it out of love."

"That's not love, Eva."

"There are lots of kinds of love. It was a twisted kind I never want to encounter again, but it was love all the same. I think you know what it means to kill in order to protect."

Jim's stomach flipped. "That's entirely different. I've never felt the need to kill someone I'm trying to protect. That's something else painted up as love."

Eva dropped her gaze. "Regardless, Tophe won't try it again. When I left him to search for you, we were working as partners. He may be waiting for us even now."

Jim let out a heavy breath and rolled his eyes over her head.

She leaned her weight onto his chest and turned her cheek to the side. "I never want to be apart from you again after this. I don't want to be here any more than you do."

He shifted her to the right, off his bruise, and tightened an arm around her good side, resting his chin on the top of her head.

"How about you keep my pistol pointed at him the whole time?" she asked. "The sooner we resolve this, the sooner we go home."

Jim scanned the tree line. He thought about what she would do if he refused her outright and knew she would feel forced to break her promise to him.

"I'll use your bow, notsaʔka. Pistols are almost pointless."

Chapter 25

Eva

Pump jumped them to a sheltered spot where they could view the rendezvous unseen. From their crouched position, he glowered beside Eva, radiating disapproval.

She pursed her lips, narrowing her eyes to slits. "You can go home, Pump."

"I should," he replied, nearly spitting, but didn't move. He just stared straight ahead.

Eva peered out over the prairie and deep into the grove of trees where Tophe should be. He was there now, pacing. She bumped her good shoulder into Jim and directed his gaze with her chin.

"I see him," he said, arrow nocked and ready.

Eva caught the older man's eye. "Pump, if you would be so kind."

When they emerged, they were still too far, but close enough for Tophe to notice them.

"Closer, please," Eva said. When Pump stonewalled her, she strode across the open sendero, and Jim crow-hopped to catch up.

Tophe ran to her but skidded to a stop when Jim raced in front and drew back his bowstring.

Jim's buckskin shirt filled Eva's vision, and rather than push him out of the way, she tilted to the side to see around him. Releasing the elbow she cradled to touch him would have hurt too much.

Tophe cocked his pistol. "Who's this?"

Eva stepped around Jim, and Jim frowned at her. "This is my husband," she said.

"Does he have a name?"

The words clung to the tip of her tongue, afraid to come out.

Jim shifted his weight and lifted his chin. "James McCullough," he said before she had a chance to decide it was safe.

"Hello, again," Tophe said, craning his neck to address Pump behind her. As her partner studied Jim, nobody moved. After a long pause, Tophe broke the silence and said to Eva, "I caught him. Come see." He turned, lowering his pistol, and walked back into the trees.

Jim eased his tension on the bow and glanced down at her. She followed Tophe.

Ephrem lay hog-tied and gagged at the foot of a red oak. The crown of his head oozed blood.

"Why didn't you kill him?" Eva circled the captive, silencing the small voice in her heart that reminded her she was not a murderer.

On a stone nearby, Tophe had dumped the contents of the man's pockets and his weapons. "I got to thinking it would be better to take him back for questioning. I went to camp to get some rope, et voilà. He was trying to steal a Mexican uniform." Tophe laughed and gave him a swift boot to the side. "Camp was the last place I would have looked for him."

The prisoner groaned and shouted something unintelligible through his gag.

"Is that your blood or someone else's?" Tophe asked, pointing at Eva's shoulder.

"Mine."

Tophe took a step toward her.

Jim tensed. "That's close enough."

Her partner froze.

"I think we should kill him," Eva said. The man on the ground protested, but all ignored him. "Otherwise, it'll be the Abyss for him." Compassion. Self-defense. Protecting her family and friends. She didn't need more to justify a quick execution here.

Tophe shrugged. "I have no problem with tossing him in the Abyss. That's where he was going to send us."

"What happens if the Elders think you know too much now?"

Tophe cast his eyes to the grass and chewed his lip. When he lifted his head, he said, "You should go back with me to the sanctum to see the doctor."

Pump raised Eva's pistol, and Jim drew the bowstring to his cheek again. Tophe put his hands in the air.

Unsurprised by the suggestion, Eva pondered for a moment. The sanctum held no immediate threat to her because the Elders were ignorant of her apostasy and betrayals. Her cracked collarbone and the tracker in her arm — those were problems more easily solved there, and she did not doubt her ability to escape and return to Jim once treated.

Less consciously, though she knew Axis Mundi could no longer be home, her broken body yearned for the safe, familiar harbor and the faces of her friends. She wanted to say goodbye. *Needed* to say goodbye to those she loved. With the gift of a few days, she would have the chance to bid a silent farewell.

"Yes," Eva said.

"No!" Pump and Jim said in unison. "And hell no," Jim said to Tophe.

Eva turned to Jim. "I will get excellent medical care where I come from. Better than here. I can even bring back food and supplies. To you, it will seem like the same instant from when I leave to when I return, and I will be completely healed."

"But what will the time feel like for you?" Jim asked.

"A couple of months."

"Enough time for plenty of terrible things to happen." He glared back at Tophe.

Tophe held his stare, unflinching. "Nothing terrible will happen to her."

Jim jabbed a finger toward Eva's neck. "Nothing?"

At the reminder, Tophe turned bright red. "I don't need to explain myself to you."

"Oh, but you do." Jim's chest expanded, and Eva shivered at his emotionless face, recognizing the mask.

"I… I thought it was the best thing, but I couldn't do it."

"And what happens when you get the courage to follow through?"

"I won't. I can't. Not to Eva." Tophe swung his attention to her, then walked over to Ephrem and kicked him in the head, knocking him out.

"Tophe!" Eva said.

He returned to her and lowered his voice, ignoring the arrow point in his chest. "If we take him back with us," he said, throwing a hand toward the Tebaki, "he is your clear alibi. I won't have to lie to the Elders. Enrique's mistake was searching for answers to questions he shouldn't have been asking. We will be bringing valuable intelligence back to Lux Libera."

"Enrique thought he was doing the same thing."

"No… Yes… but only because I urged him to, and he sought it out." Tophe pointed at Eva's bruised temple. "This information literally attacked us unawares. Also, how else do we account for our failure? If I go back alone, they will send people after you. And when they find you, they'll find him." He shifted his focus to Jim. "And maybe him," he said, gesturing at Pump. "And that baby," he said, reaching toward her stomach, but not touching it.

Eva pictured the eternal darkness the Guardian would enter and set her loved ones next to him. She had to choose.

"She's not going to be able to hide her pregnancy for another two months," Jim said.

"We'll be granted leave to a sanctioned location on another timeline for her to recover," Tophe said.

"When I return alone, they'll send people to that timeline instead of this one."

"You won't try to convince her to stay?"

Tophe gave him a long look, running his eyes up and down Jim's face and chest. "Eva tells me you're real — that you have a soul the same as we do."

When Jim blew out slowly, Eva let go of her elbow to grasp his arm, just in case he didn't get his temper under control. Pain shot to the top of her head and radiated down her spine.

"I've seen enough that I have a lot of my own thinking to do," Tophe said. "If she won't return to her old life, I want to know she is safe here."

Eva tugged Jim to face her. "I will return to you. I promise. Nothing will stop me. Tophe's plan has a better chance of keeping us safe than if I don't go back with him."

"Is his word worth anything?" Jim asked.

In her peripheral vision, Tophe clenched his fists.

"Yes," Eva said.

Jim scanned Tophe's face. "I want your word that you will return her and leave us in peace, including Pump and my child."

"You have it."

More exhausted than she could ever recall, Eva leaned her forehead onto Jim's chest.

"This is the last time you leave me," he whispered in her ear. "The last time. Do you hear me?"

As she gazed up at him, he placed his forehead on hers. He cupped her face with both his hands, and she closed her eyes. When she looked at Tophe, he was watching them, but his thoughts seemed to be elsewhere. The shadow behind his eyes flew away as he refocused on her.

Ephrem stirred, and Tophe bent to untie his legs and hauled him to his feet. The man swayed, his head drooping.

"Ready?" Tophe asked.

She glanced back at Pump and blew him a kiss.

He returned it without smiling, skepticism seeping from every pore. "Come back."

Eva nodded.

With her good hand, she pulled Jim's head down for a kiss. "What would you like me to bring you to eat?"

A slow grin spread over his face. "Meat. Lots of it."

"I'll bring you a buffet, my love."

"Does that have four legs or two?"

"It has all the legs," she said, laughing at his confusion.

After he uncurled his grip on her waist, she cuffed the Guardian's other arm and looked back over her shoulder. Tophe touched the tree, and they were gone.

Chapter 26

Jim

Eva's and Tophe's bodies flipped in place and strode toward them. To Jim's eyes, the captive simply vanished. Eva's skin glowed, and she moved with ease, joy lighting her face as she ran the last steps to him. He caught her in a bear hug and sagged under the weight of all the bags she carried, and she consumed him with her kisses. When she allowed him a breath, he combed his fingers through her hair, yellow as the wood of a new bow.

"All one color. The real me." Eva's smile dazzled him.

Tophe coughed behind her and lowered his own burdens to the ground.

"Stay with us and eat," she said, reaching out her hand to him.

In answer to the invitation, her partner eyed Jim's bow hand.

Jim couldn't believe what he had just witnessed, that what they had said would happen actually had. He hadn't had a chance to miss her for even a second. Delayed relief pushed generous feelings and ingrained etiquette to the forefront. "Yes, please. Stay.

Share our meal," he said, forcing himself to lean the bow against a rock.

Tophe smiled, cutting the tension. "I was hoping you would say that. You'll need help eating all she's brought. Every day, she thought of another dish to bring you."

"We should jump someplace farther from Goliad," Pump said, releasing Eva from an embrace. "Preferably one with water."

As soon as they deemed it safe, miles from the presidio, Eva spread a quilt and laid out strange containers nearly as clear as glass.

Disoriented and exhausted, Jim watched his wife from where he sat. Everything had happened too quickly. He had faced death less than an hour ago and just wanted to go home. If he didn't need to eat, he would have insisted they leave immediately. Eva chattered as if his near-execution had faded into the distant past. He knew, for her, much time had passed, but even Pump seemed to cast off his previous concerns with ease.

To distract himself, Jim picked up the nearest object, and it gave way under his fingers. When he squeezed, the lid popped. A rich, warm smell puffed out, and his stomach rumbled. A rivulet of saliva dripped from his lower lip, and he checked that no one had seen it as he swiped it away.

Eva held out a knife, fork, and plate to him. All he wanted to do was scoop the contents out with his bare hands, but he set the container down to take what she offered.

"There's beef tenderloin, roasted potatoes, creamed spinach, corn, fried chicken, gravy, coconut shrimp, roasted vegetables, coleslaw, quinoa salad," she said, pointing to each thing. "That's sushi."

Jim's eyes followed her fingers to the colorful circles. They didn't look like food at all.

"You're not going to want that," Pump said. He loomed over the blanket with his own plate in hand. "It's disgusting."

"No, it's not!" Eva said. "It's delicious. Don't prejudice him."

"I'll try it," Jim said, holding up his palm. "I don't care. I just want to eat."

"Be sure to spread a lot of that green paste on top. Makes it taste better. Don't be shy about it."

"Gah! Don't listen to him," Eva said. "Try a little bit before you do that. It's… what's the right word? Hot's not the right word… Spicy?"

"It liberates the sinuses," Pump said.

Jim widened his eyes, more bewildered than anything.

She pointed at Pump. "You need to be quiet."

Pump swallowed a toothy grin.

Eva listed off the other dishes, but Jim stopped listening. From another bag, she withdrew desserts: chocolate pie with a graham cracker crust and apple crumble. Eva took his plate from him and put a little of everything on it, and Jim grinned with relief to get down to the business of eating.

As they ate, they pressed their thighs together, and Eva leaned her head on his shoulder between bites. Jim stuffed his mouth and asked for reminders on what some things were called. The sushi with its sauces was unlike anything he had tasted before.

"This is good," he said to Pump, pointing at his full cheek. "What's wrong with you?"

"It's raw fish. You'd like anything in your state."

Jim paused, jaw locked.

Eva put a hand over her mouth. "I didn't think about the taboos. I'm sorry." Her eyes darted over the containers and down at his plate, her cheeks reddening. "Shrimp comes from the water, too. Nothing was made with hog fat, though."

He forced his mouth to chew again, then ate faster. It was the best desperation food he had ever tasted. "No, it's good."

Eva searched his face.

"Really," he said, taking her hand and kissing it. He didn't want to let go of her.

Pump shrugged. "Suit yourself."

"Let me see your shoulder," Jim said, changing the subject.

Eva pulled the embroidered square neck of her blouse aside.

Jim ran his finger over the scar and the slight bump where her bones had reknit. He brought his lips to her ear. "This deserves a tattoo."

She blushed.

When he caught sight of a new scar, he rolled her arm. "What's this?"

"That's where the doctor removed a T'ibek'a beacon. It would have drawn our enemies to us. Another reason I needed to return. I didn't want the device to remain in this world."

He lifted her arm and kissed the spot. "Anything else I don't know about?"

Eva gazed up into the canopy, pondering. "No, I think that's it."

"I like your new dress, too." Jim fingered her patterned skirt and raised it to admire her Nʉmʉ-style, knee-high beaded boots. "More beautiful than the day I found you." His world narrowed to her face, and her eyes fixed on his. He kissed her on the mouth, not caring if the other men saw.

"That reminds me! I brought you new clothes and a set for myself." Eva stood, digging in one of the bags. "I commissioned these from Nʉmʉ artists." She held up a beaded and fringed shirt, tabbed leggings, a scarlet and embroidered breechcloth, and fringed moccasins. One after another, she carried them to him, and he ran his hand over the exquisite beadwork and dyed flares.

Most excited to find she had included shoes for him, he dusted the last of the mud from his feet and tried on the moccasins. His big toe scrunched a smidge, but he could stretch them.

Eva bit her lip.

"They fit perfectly."

She sighed, her shoulders relaxing. "I really, really hope the clothes fit."

He held them against his body. "They will be perfect, too. Thank you. I'll be the best-dressed man in the village." He tallied the effort required for all these things. "This took longer than two months. How much time has passed for you?"

Eva tucked her lips and peeked back at Tophe.

Tophe dropped his eyes to his plate.

"The artist and her husband had many of the items already finished and for sale," she said. "It was just a few extra weeks."

Jim focused on her rounded belly for the first time, and his heart sank.

"I didn't want to come home empty-handed," she said, touching his shoulder. "Not when I realized all I could do for us." Eva's face shone with devotion for him, dispelling his unworthy suspicions of her, but he still felt robbed. Though flint sparked against steel in his gut, he let it go and scattered the tinder. It didn't make any difference now.

He noticed Tophe staring again, and the hairs on the back of his neck rose. Not being acquainted with the man, he didn't know how to read his face, but a deep sadness overshadowed whatever other emotions swirled beneath the man's features.

Eva folded the clothes and re-wrapped them. "I have lots of beautiful, useful gifts, even some not invented yet, for our family and friends."

Jim's curiosity was piqued when Pump said, "Is that wise, Eva?"

"Why not?"

"Timeline integrity, et cetera?"

"Who cares? I mean, really? There's an infinity of Evas out there who brought only appropriate items back and decided not to do anything to change the fate of their new people. This feels right to me."

"And your promise to the Guardians?" Tophe asked.

"They're dead. Besides, my very presence here… this baby… I've already started a new line. We get to choose. It's all yet to be decided."

Pump's lips puckered, but then he bounced a dismissive shoulder. "Maybe so."

As Jim laced Eva's fingers through his and kissed the knuckles of her hand, he could see the unobstructed path home, but he wouldn't celebrate until they were seated in his brother's lodge. He laid back, his shrunken stomach bursting, wanting to eat more, but knowing he shouldn't. Eva took his plate and finished what he couldn't, and he watched in stunned silence as she picked over the remains of the feast for more.

"We should wait until tonight to leave and steal all the horses," he said. With food on his belly, Jim could think through the advantages of a delay. He imagined himself entering the village in his new finery, Eva mounted behind him, and leading every cavalry and pack horse the combined Mexican and Texian armies boasted.

"Horses don't like to enter portals," Eva said. "I learned that the hard way. If we steal more than one, we'll be riding them all the way home and through a war zone. Even if I could get them all in, I wouldn't have the strength for that many."

"I'm still amazed you got Poops A Lot to cooperate at all," Pump said to Eva. "And that was before I taught you how to skim."

"Never mind, then," Jim said, eyelids drooping. "I guess you won't be the key to our staggering future wealth."

Eva laughed. "I wouldn't go that far. I have a few other tricks up my sleeve."

On a raised elbow, Jim scanned the horizon for threats until exhaustion pulled him back to the blanket, and he thought he might let himself take a nap — just a little one.

Without warning, Tophe shot to his feet, and Jim bolted upright in response, every muscle tense again. His stomach threatened to revolt, and he shoved its contents back down with a firm hand.

"Sorry, I didn't mean to startle you," Tophe said. "I should take my leave."

"No, not yet!" Eva pushed herself to stand and grabbed his wrist.

A hard knot formed in Jim's chest as his wife begged Tophe not to go.

"You can choose to stay," she said. "There can be a place for you in this world. We can still travel — wherever we want."

Jim's mouth fell open. Her words shocked him, lancing him through the heart, and the pain froze him in place.

Tophe sighed. "We've been over this."

"I know, but there must be timelines where you choose to stay. Let this be one of them. We can decide later what to do about Lux Libera."

"If what you believe is true, then there are lines where we never got separated and others where you returned with me when we reunited in El Copano. It's not meant to be. This world has chosen for us." He walked to the nearest cottonwood tree.

Eva followed him. "It's not fate, Tophe. You can choose for yourself. You can be free. I chose this!"

"Then you chose for both of us." Bitterness dripped from Tophe's tongue, and in rapid, furious answer, she launched into a stream of French.

Anger propelled Jim to his feet. Unsure if she was having second thoughts, he closed the distance between them and placed a hand on her elbow. She ignored him, and the pitch and speed of her pleas increased. When Tophe kissed her on the forehead, Jim sucked in a breath, using every ounce of self-discipline to resist ripping his wife from the man's hands.

Her true friend cupped her shoulders and held his lips to her brow until her words slowed to a trickle and stopped.

When Tophe whispered into her ear, drilling his eyes into Jim's own, a flash of heat ran up Jim's neck and flowed across his face at the stranger's direct challenge. His hand itched to pull his blade, and a dimming awareness of cultural differences struggled to keep him in check.

If his wife had grown up Nʉmʉ, this man would already be dead. A man kissing another man's woman was bad enough, but brothers, even adopted ones, never kissed their sisters. Sisters could be killed for shaming a brother in such a way. He'd be hard-pressed to name a stricter taboo, and blood roared in his ears at the boundaries being crossed right before his very eyes.

Jim's rational mind shouted to be heard over his pride and upbringing, and a chant droned in his head.

True friend. Not a lover. Celibate. He's leaving. True Friend. Not a lover. Celibate. He's leaving. His heart paced like a bear at the end of a short chain.

As she whispered back, Eva cried, and a tear slid down Tophe's cheek. He screwed his eyes shut, then hugged her, and she wrapped her arms around him, her shoulders shaking. Jim's hand rose of its own accord from her elbow to cuff her upper arm.

Tophe let go, putting space between them. Face solemn, he reached up to her forehead, and with his index finger, he drew the first stroke of a large X, then hovered at the crosshatch for a moment as if unwilling to complete the mark. "You, Eva, have forsaken the Admonishments and are excommunicated. Dead to Lux Libera."

She choked on a sob and stared up into his face.

His voice fell to a whisper. "But not to me, ma crotte. Never to me." He kissed her on each cheek and once more on her forehead, then sought Jim's eye.

At Jim's glare, Tophe faltered for a second, but his own eye hardened. "I am not your enemy. Or your rival. I honor my vows still, as did Eva. Her heart and loyalties belong only to you. I will keep your location secret. You will not be found."

Jim inclined his head. "Thank you," he said through gritted teeth. Tophe's words did little to squash his jealousy, and if he could have formed a portal himself, he would have pushed the man out of his world.

After one last embrace and lingering gaze, Tophe relinquished her hand and disappeared into the tree.

Jim held tight for another moment, afraid she would follow him, but then released Eva and shook out his arms with an exhale, knowing he had to trust her at some point. She could leave him at any time, and the naked truth struck fear to his very core.

Unmoored, he glanced back at Pump, who lifted a brow and pursed his lips. Jim's chest expanded at his mentor's validation; he had not been out of line. Pump hadn't liked the display either.

Long past when Tophe would have returned, if she would ever see him again in this timeline, Eva stood watching, and Jim's temper settled, certain he had seen the last of him. He covered the ferocious coals in his heart with ash.

After several minutes, he encircled Eva and rested his hands on her belly. Flowers scented her hair, and he pulled her to himself, complete once again, if not completely whole. His pierced heart still bled.

Under his fingers, something pressed against the surface and disappeared. Eva moved his hand down the side of her stomach, and he felt the baby again, then kissed the crown of her head, wishing he had felt all the previous kicks he had missed while she was gone.

"I chose you. Only you," Eva said. "Months ago. That never changed. It never will change." Eva wiped at her cheeks with the palms of her hand and turned to him.

"You begged him to stay."

"As you would have begged Kuhtu."

He cast himself and his true friend in the scene he had just witnessed and smirked at the absurdity. "No. I wouldn't have."

Eva lowered her gaze. "Let's go home."

Chapter 27

Eva

The imprint of Tophe's mark on her forehead seared Eva's soul. She couldn't believe she would never see him again. When Eva had left her birth family, she hadn't known what she was doing, but Tophe's leaving tore her heart out, even more than she had expected. Not a day had gone by that she hadn't tried to convince him to join her in this world. To live in the village, to live with Pump and the Anglos, to make his own way, she didn't care which, as long as it was here.

Heartbroken, she turned from the tree, but Jim's phantom fingers still gripped her arm. Unblemished skin rebuked her when she pulled back her sleeve to check for a bruise, reminding her of her promise never to make Jim feel the need to hold her in place by force. As she found his face, she saw his jaw had re-tightened at her inspection of where his hand had been.

"I keep my promises," he said, eyes sparking. Without another word, he bent to pack their baggage. His statement left Eva hollowed and rooted to the ground for a moment, unable to respond.

Pump watched her, impassive. At her approach, he drew a breath to speak in hushed tones. "I warned you. You're lucky he didn't kill him."

"You understand, though, don't you?" Eva's voice cracked. "Could you watch your entire family leave you forever without crying?"

Pump's eyes softened. "No, honey," he said, pulling her into a hug.

Fresh tears sprang to her eyes, and she sobbed silently into his chest. "I had hoped he could be free."

"Freedom often means choosing your own chains." Though Pump offered no further words of comfort, he rubbed her back. When she pushed away several minutes later, she thought she might be able to face Jim.

All their bags sat in a neat pile, and her husband was inspecting each of her arrows. The two broken shafts from when the ball had gone through her quiver lay at his feet, but he had saved the points. He raised shuttered eyes. "Ready?"

Eva swallowed. "Yes."

Pump skimmed them up the coast. When they arrived in the woods outside Pump's relatives' house, Jim grasped his mentor's arm and clapped him on the shoulder. "I will visit you this winter when we camp near the Anglo settlements."

"Eva can bring you anytime you want."

The corners of Jim's mouth lifted. "True."

"Just don't visit me with a raiding party," Pump said, chuckling.

A real smile spread to Jim's eyes. "Never."

Pump darted his gaze at Eva. "Look for me in Nacogdoches. Send Eva in her cloth dress to ask after me. Don't go into town yourself until I make sure the community is safe for you. I don't know who from San Felipe will settle there."

Jim took a deep breath and dipped his chin in acknowledgment.

Pump placed a fatherly kiss on each of their foreheads and headed for the house. They watched as he mounted the steps and opened the front door. Shrieks of joy spilled out into the yard.

Happy to have returned Pump to his family, Eva grinned up at Jim, but he turned dull eyes to her.

"Let's go," he said in Comanche. "I'm beyond ready to be home."

Chastened, she formed her hands in front of them, and they stepped through. Eva skimmed across the Piney Woods but stopped at the edge for Jim to take his bearings. As they traveled, Eva couldn't help thinking of Tophe and the time she and her partner had spent over the last weeks learning to skim together and building strength.

Unfamiliar with this country, Jim said he knew only to head west, horizon by horizon, until he recognized something. Otherwise, they didn't speak. When they came across a familiar river, he took a stick and drew Eva a map. In no time at all, she glimpsed their village and pulled back to a thicket of live oaks several miles from it.

Jim set down the bags he carried. "You're not going to be able to carry all that by yourself," he said, frowning.

"I can try to trick a couple of our horses from the herd into my portal. If I do them one at a time, I should have enough strength to skim and not jump. We'll have to wait until after dark, though."

"Yes." Jim continued to stare at the bags. "I just want to be home," he said in a monotone. "Right now. I don't even care if I enter the village on foot and carrying baggage."

Eva's heart stumbled with misgivings. "Let's just leave what I can't carry here. We'll come back for it tomorrow with horses."

"No. I'll care tomorrow and wish we had waited. What's one more day?" Without looking up, Jim cleared the ground with his foot, and Eva took that as her cue to gather wood. Together, they blew the fire to life.

"I want you to eat more," she said, pulling out the leftovers from their feast. Jim didn't respond but shifted from his knees to sit crisscross. They ate straight from the containers in silence, and she laid her hand on his thigh. After a time, he curled his fingers around her palm.

"I missed you," she said. "So much."

He squeezed her hand, but the fire held his attention.

When he still didn't respond, she asked, "Do you think I slept with Tophe?"

"No. Worse. That he has your heart."

Eva's brow creased. "But I'm here. With you." The wood popped, and a gust of wind sent embers into the air. "Tophe was my only family. More than anyone else in Lux Libera. He watched out for me like a mother, protected me like a father, fought by my side like a brother. He was my true friend and more, but never my lover. What can I say that will make you believe me?"

"I don't disbelieve you, notsaʔka. It just hurts."

"I'm not jealous or hurt by your love for your family." She narrowed her eyes. "Or Tʉe Tseenaʔ."

At her sister's name, he jerked his head to look at her. "That's different."

"It is different. I've never slept with Tophe."

He frowned at her veiled accusation.

"And I'm surprised you were so angry. I thought you trusted me."

Jim's brows drew down in confusion. "Why in the world would you be surprised by my jealousy? The man was kissing all over your face!" His fists clenched.

"He's always kissed me on the face. The French in his birth line kiss everyone on the face. He would have kissed you on the face if you had been his friend."

Jim turned to the fire and opened his hands, flexing his fingers, but she could tell he heard her.

"Your heart is big enough to hold all the people you love. So is mine." She took his hand and placed it on her chest. "Tophe doesn't replace you, and you don't replace Tophe. Let me mourn my partner. I grieve as if he is dead. That time in my life is over, but he will always be precious to me. The love I feel for him is different from the love I feel for you. It always has been. Both kinds of love fit inside my heart, but only you are at the center of it." A tear crept down her cheek. "I chose you. I could leave and join Tophe at any time, but you are the path I now walk."

"That's my worst fear. That you will leave me someday." His voice sank so low she almost asked him to repeat himself.

She moved to kneel before him, the flames at her back. "I need you, Jim. You are the air I breathe. My lifeline is twined with yours. When I look, I see it glowing between us. My line only ever ran parallel to Tophe's, never joined together like ours." She kissed the palm of his hand. "I drove Tophe up the wall talking about you non-stop. Getting back to you filled my every thought. I will never leave you. I promise. Even when you are old and wrinkly and stinky. I begged the artists to work day and night so I could return to you sooner."

"No set of clothes is worth the time I lost with you. With our child." He held her belly in his hands. "Tophe got that time with you instead. I want it back."

At the look on Jim's face, Eva's heart broke into four quarters. "I'm sorry." She sought the right words. They sounded like an excuse, but she said them anyway because they were the truth. "I knew I could never make you something so beautiful. I wanted you to be able to return home proud and not ragged." With her vision blurring, she cupped his battered face. "I'm the reason you…" She ran her fingers down his body. Unable to finish her thought, she picked up both of his hands and bowed over them, bathing them with her tears. "I'm sorry."

As she pressed his palms against her cheeks, he didn't reply. Several beats passed before he bent down to kiss the back of her head. "It's not your fault I ended up in Goliad."

"Yes. It is."

He pulled his hands free and lifted her. "Come here," he said, opening his lap.

"I don't think I'll fit."

"We'll make it work."

She straddled him, and he wrapped his arms around her. The baby kicked between them. Wonder lit Jim's eyes, and he pulled her closer to induce another kick. "Hello, baby."

Eva leaned back so she could breathe, smiling, then pushed his hair from his face and turned solemn once again. "I love you. Only you. And I will never leave you." She dropped her eyes. "I would make it so Goliad had never happened if I could." With a ragged sigh, she spoke the hardest words of all. "I will never speak the name of Tophe again, as if he were truly dead."

For a long moment, Jim pierced her with his gaze, and when he was satisfied with what he saw, he nodded. Tears rolled down her cheeks, but he touched his forehead to her own. "What's done is done, Eva. We will both heal, your heart and my body. As Pump said, it's nothing a few good meals won't fix. What matters is we're home safe together, and we love each other. We will start fresh tomorrow."

In answer, she kissed the bruises on his brow, cheekbones, and chin. Jim pressed his head into her chest and sighed, every muscle seeming to relax. They held each other, and the sun moved overhead. After a time, he asked, "Even when I'm old and wrinkly and stinky?"

"Even then. Case in point."

Jim sniffed himself and laughed. "I have never smelled so bad in my life."

"Swim?"

"I think that would be a very good idea."

Eva jumped them to the nearest creek. Without hesitation, Jim stripped and waded into a shallow pool, but Eva remained standing on the bank.

"Aren't you coming in?"

"It's cold. Besides, I'm clean. I had a shower this morning."

"Get in."

"Uh… no."

"Don't make me come over there and get you."

"In your weakened state? I think I'm pretty safe."

Jim arched an eyebrow and strode back toward her. She giggled until she realized he was serious, then she turned to run. Jim caught her under the arms and scooped her legs.

"Oof, you're heavier than I remember."

If Eva hadn't been pregnant, she would have taken him to the ground, but she resigned herself to getting wet. Water from his damp body soaked through her clothes. "At least undress me first."

"Gladly," Jim said, setting her down. He pulled her shirt over her head and unlaced her skirts. Eva dropped her chemise on the grass and shivered. Jim stepped back to take a better look at her new body.

At his serious face, she bit her lip, unsure if he still found her attractive. When her eyes traveled down his body, his reaction reassured her, and she smiled. "Like what you see?"

Jim nodded, a wide grin spreading across his face. "You're beautiful." He moved closer and cupped her larger breasts.

As he trailed kisses down her neck, she said, "You need to wash first."

Jim groaned but took her hand and pulled her into the creek. Eva squealed and hissed as the height of the water rose between her legs. Once she acclimated, she helped Jim rub sand over his greasy, grimy skin, and he floated on his back while she scrubbed his hair. He moaned in contentment as she massaged his scalp, then she planted a kiss on his forehead when she was done.

He let his feet fall and wrung his hair out behind him. "Now, where was I?"

Eva pointed to her neck. "Somewhere around here."

Jim grinned and closed the space between them. "I think I want to start here, though," he said and kissed her mouth. His hands explored her broader hips and rounder behind as she trailed her own kisses. Avoiding his musket wound, she spread her hands over his ropey chest, then fingered the new, pink skin encircling his neck. He reached under her stomach and drew her onto him.

Her surprised gasp stopped him.

"I'm okay," she said. "Pregnancy makes me more sensitive. In a good way."

His eyes lit at her words, and he made her gasp again.

"It's almost too much."

"Is that even possible?"

Eva giggled. "Apparently," she said, feeling the water flow around them.

He spun them in a lazy circle, putting the current at his back. When she looked into his eyes, she still saw doubts, pain, and fear. Eva kept forgetting she'd had months to recover, but he had faced execution that very morning. She brought her lips next to his ear. "I chose you. I chose you. I chose you. I love you. I love you. I love you." Even with those soft words, his eyes filled with the firing squad, revealing his injured soul, and the guilt nearly drowned her. "I will never, ever put you last again. Never." She could rattle off a dozen reasons and excuses, but at the end of the day, she had taken risks with his life. "I promise."

"Don't make promises you can't keep, Eva." When she flinched, he said. "I know, in my head, you made the right choices, and some things were out of your control, but my heart feels betrayed. It just needs time to catch up."

"No… maybe I would make the same choices over and over again for all the same right reasons, but neither Francisca nor even my partner was worth saving over you. I can live a life without my true friend, but I couldn't live a life without you. If I had found you dead, I would have joined you in the grave."

Jim gazed at the well of her neck, then set his cheek against her breast. "I would not have wished for you there, notsaʔka." His arms pulled her tight, and she knew her heart beat in his ear.

When he raised his head, she lowered her eyes and her voice. "Please forgive me, Jim. I will never make you feel that way again."

With her words, the last of the doubt and fear melted from his eyes, leaving only the pain. He reached a dripping hand to the back of her head and met her lips with a deep, hungry kiss. "You were already forgiven," he said when he released her. "All we need now is time." Gently, he rocked her hips.

Though he warmed her, a shadow fell over the creek as the sun dropped behind the trees, and her teeth chattered. "Let's go back to the fire."

"Only if we're going to pick up where we left off."

"Of course," she said, pecking his nose.

Eva skimmed them back to their campsite and fed the coals while Jim built them a bed of cedar boughs and blankets. They snuggled, and she rubbed her icy feet along his calves.

"You will regret that if you keep doing it," he said, pinning her ankles under his legs. "It will be much harder for us to have any fun."

"Being cold in the creek didn't stop you."

"I didn't say impossible," he said, winking at her. "Your body keeps me plenty warm. Your feet, though, are another story."

Eva tugged a foot free and darted it toward his thigh.

"Woman!" he said, catching it.

Eva relented and apologized with her hands.

"That's much better," Jim said. "Please keep doing that instead."

Once she warmed and he was ready, she eased herself on top of him. She tried to lean down to kiss him, but the baby pushed the air from her lungs. "I can't reach you."

Jim's eyes smoldered. "But I can watch you." He ran his hands over her belly and down her hips. "You go the pace you need. I will follow."

Eva rode him, shocked by the depth of sensation in her new body. His eyes drank in her movements, and she climaxed before he did.

"Again," he said, his voice heavy with longing.

Within moments, pleasure radiated through her core to the tips of her fingers and toes, and he joined her. She tilted her head back and saw a pink and orange sky blazing above them. She wanted this very moment to last forever.

When she curled next to him, he sighed heavily, clutching her as if he could pull her inside his own body. "I feel whole again."

"Me, too." The baby flipped and kicked in quick succession. While he kissed the back of her hair, Eva took Jim's hand from her breast to chase the movements. A large knot surfaced against her skin, and she raced his hand to the spot. "I think that's the baby's bottom. Oh, and there's a foot. Push there."

Jim pressed the tiny rectangle she indicated and was rewarded with a responding kick. Joy bubbled from his lips.

"She just started kicking where someone else could feel this week." Eva stopped herself from saying, "You didn't miss that much."

"She?"

"Or he. We could get a scan to tell us what we're having. It's probably a good idea, anyway."

"What?"

"In the future, they can see the baby inside a woman without hurting her."

Jim's eyes rounded. "Truly?"

"Yes."

"Haʔii! I don't know what I think about that."

"It's a good thing."

As Jim's clean scent flowed around her, they settled into silence, listening to the fire crackle and the wind blow.

Without realizing she had dozed, she opened her eyes when he shook her awake, and full night cloaked the campsite. The remaining embers flickered.

"Let's get our horses," Jim said.

"I'll go by myself. You sleep."

"No, never again."

Eva knew better than to argue but found she didn't even want to, happy to stay connected to him. They dressed, and as soon as they were ready, she skimmed them to the herd and searched, but it was too dark. She dropped them back at camp.

"We should have scouted while there was daylight," she said.

"What do you mean? We passed over our horses twice. Take me back." He described the exact place she should go, and she opened a new portal. After she set them in the middle of the herd, Jim cooed and ran his hands over the startled animals. He put his mouth against her ear. "You definitely needed me."

Jim selected a saddle-broken gelding, slipped one of the new halters Eva had brought over its head, and, after he mounted, hauled her up behind him. Eva opened a portal, and he kicked the horse forward. It refused to move. Nearby, a herder huddled under his blanket atop a horse, sound asleep.

After letting a full minute pass, Eva pressed Jim's shoulder down to whisper in his ear. "We're going to have to make him." She slid off, took the lead rope, and pulled. The horse dug in its heels.

Jim huffed. "Have I taught you nothing?" He landed on cat's feet next to her, lifted the rope from her hands, and stroked the gelding's neck for a moment. "Take my hand and open your portal. Then, we're going to calmly intend to walk forward without paying any attention to the horse. He will follow."

Like magic, the gelding trailed Jim into the doorway, and she returned them to camp.

"You wouldn't be able to get him to follow you through again," Eva said.

"You're probably right, but that's how you lead a horse. You have to act like you're worth following. Confident. I know I've taught you that."

"You have, but it's harder than it looks."

"It feels strange to steal my own horses." He sniffed at a thought. "We could pick off single horses all day, every day, year-round. Maybe you *will* be the key to our staggering wealth."

"We'll see," she said, laughing.

They collected the second horse without incident and went back to bed. Eva rested her belly against Jim's side. As if he had forgotten something, he stretched to feel for the strung bow and quiver and pulled them closer while she murmured a complaint.

"Sorry. I'm finally starting to think straight again." He had her roll over and seated her bottom in the crease of his hips. After a moment, she felt him rising again, and when he wanted to enter, she shifted, opening herself. Connected once again, he settled. "That's better." He nibbled her ear, then kissed the back of her neck a final time before going back to sleep.

At first light, they both woke up, anxious to finish their journey. After eating, they dressed in their new clothes, and Eva brushed and braided his hair.

Jim beamed at her. "Now, that is a beautiful dress," he said, his eyes running from the tips of her boots to her neckline.

"Thank you," she said, grinning back at him.

Jim turned his attention to contemplating their baggage and lack of a pack saddle but rigged a series of rope loops that would make do. Once all was ready, he sat Eva behind him and turned the gelding's head toward the village.

"How are we going to explain all these new things?" He reached back and jiggled her thigh. "For one, people know you can't sew. And… your pregnancy is further along… your hair is different."

Eva tightened her grip around his waist. "I think we tell your family who I am."

In surprise, he glanced sidelong over his shoulder at her. "I'm not so sure about that."

"Secrets only breed trouble. I'm tired of pretending to be something I'm not."

Jim turned his head to the front, silent for a beat. "We'll discuss. Let me think on it," he said, and Eva smiled.

When they crested the last hill, Jim whooped to see the clusters of kahnis following the river at their feet. Sentries galloped toward them, and he raised his arms in greeting. Eva scanned the village, found Ohayaa and Tʉe Tseenaʔ walking a path with Wokweesi, and waved to get their attention. Their lu-lu-lu's laid a carpet before them.

"Welcome home," she said into Jim's ear.

Epilogue

Eva moaned as she strained against the pole driven into the ground near her bed and settled into a deep squat. "I can't do this. I can't do this… something… must… be… wrong." The words slipped through her lips as she struggled to hold her viscera together. Once, long ago, she had witnessed a blood eagle performed on a criminal in a Norse village, but now, she no longer needed to use her imagination to know what the man had felt when the ax had separated his ribs from his spine. Her body was splitting in two, and she could do nothing to stop it.

"Yes, you can." Tʉe Tseenaʔ's tone brooked no argument. "This is a good sign. The baby will want to come now. I'm telling you; this is the hardest part."

Ohayaa tested a heated river stone in her hand and passed it to her sister. Tʉe Tseenaʔ traded her the cooled one she had been gliding over Eva's buttocks, hips, and lower back with firm strokes and held her hand out for a second.

Eva had naively thought she would travel to a world with a hospital if the pain became too great, but she had hit a point of no return, and every fiber of her being now focused on the task at hand. She wasn't able to go anywhere. Of their own accord, her hands grasped the pole as if they could keep a force of nature from tearing her apart.

"You can do it, Younger Sister," Ohayaa said. "Every woman reaches a point where she thinks she can go no further. Your courage is being tested. Until this moment, you have been staying out of the way of your body, but it's time for you to work now." She relieved Tʉe Tseenaʔ, took Eva's buttocks between her hands, and jiggled them roughly up and down and side to side.

Tʉe Tseenaʔ shook out her arms.

A piercing shriek escaped Eva's lips. Panic clawed at her, and she wished to crawl out of her skin. Where Ohayaa's ministrations had eased her suffering earlier, now they only increased it as the contractions came, one on top of another. Caught between waves as if in an undertow, she had no chance to recover and calm herself before the next one.

Her reaction alerted Tʉe Tseenaʔ. "It's time to put you over the afterbirth pit."

Tears ran down Eva's cheeks at the thought of moving. "I can't." Her entire body shook violently.

"You must," Tʉe Tseenaʔ said. "We will help you. It's right here. Look." Her sister peeled her hands from the pole, and Ohayaa helped her turn on her heels. Tʉe Tseenaʔ held her arms and gently transferred Eva's death grip to the new staff.

Only days before, Jim had dug the hole she now straddled and built the brush arbor that shielded them from view on the outskirts of the village. With great care, he had churned and sifted the dirt at the bottom of the pit into a soft pillow.

Steamy, aromatic sage filled her nose, and Ohayaa began to sing. Without warning, Eva's body pushed with all its might. A warm liquid gushed from between her legs, soaking into the earth under her feet.

"That's good. That's just your waters." Tʉe Tseenaʔ lay on the ground to watch Eva's birth canal, but didn't touch. "Try to relax now during the break, and don't push so hard on the next one."

"I can't help it." Eva couldn't have stopped the power if she had wanted to, and she didn't want to.

"You must, or you will tear," Tʉe Tseenaʔ said, shifting her attention to Eva's face. "Listen to me, Nami. You'll want to push your baby out all at once, but your body is not ready. You *cannot* let it."

On the next push, pure energy shot through her like the very hand of God, and she screamed and trembled in awe.

"No, Eva! You need to control the power. When you yell, you send it out of your body, and then your baby doesn't move at all."

Hot fury coursed through Eva's veins at her sister's words, and the unusual use of her real name shocked her. Tʉe Tseenaʔ might as well be asking her to catch lightning in her hands and direct it where to go. On the next push, Eva dammed her mouth and sent the energy to her core, but agony leaked through her lips.

"Perfect," Tʉe Tseenaʔ said. "That's it."

Nothing else existed except her body, the power, and Tʉe Tseenaʔ's voice. Even Ohayaa's singing faded, unheard.

Finally, Tʉe Tseenaʔ said, "I see hair!"

When the power flowed down her spine again, an unexpected ring of fire ignited between her thighs.

"Ease off, Younger Sister. Ease off. That's it."

Sweat poured down her face, stinging her eyes. Ohayaa's singing returned in her ear, and when she pushed again, she allowed herself to roar.

This time, Tʉe Tseenaʔ just watched without rebuke, silent until she called her back from going too far. When the last wave passed, she said, "Put your hand down on the next push. Your baby's head is almost out."

Within moments, Eva's entire being clenched again, and her sister said, "Now, Nami! Push, push, push, with everything you've got."

Eva turned herself inside out to cross through the fiery blaze, and her baby's head fell into her hand. The excruciating pain shifted instantly to ecstasy when the shoulders cleared, and Eva giggled with wonder, shock, and joy.

"Pick him up, Younger Sister," Ohayaa said. "Your hands should be the first he feels."

He? Eva thought. All she beheld was a pure soul, and her arms shook as she scooped his bloody, creamy body up to her chest and cleaned his nose. "Hello, baby," she said. "I thought you would be a girl." They had never bothered to get a scan. Neither Jim nor she had wished to leave the village.

Her newborn's body arched rigidly at the change in his existence, and his lungs pumped fast, rhythmic cries of protest. He was both larger and smaller than she had ever imagined. "How did you fit inside me?"

"Pasahòo will be so proud," Tʉe Tseenaʔ said over the baby's cries. She crawled next to Eva and helped guide the baby's mouth to her nipple.

Eva chased the baby's lower lip, unable to connect.

"On the next cry, shove your nipple into his mouth," Tʉe Tseenaʔ said.

After several more attempts, they connected, and Eva's heart filled with triumph. She hissed the very next moment when the baby sucked. "Ow. Wow. That. Hurts."

Ohayaa chuckled. "Yes, it'll take a bit for you to toughen up, but that's normal. Eventually, it won't hurt at all."

Eva's belly contracted again, pulling stronger with each suck on her breast, and she cried out in surprise. She had forgotten she wasn't done.

Tʉe Tseenaʔ held the pulsing umbilical cord in her hand.

"Lean against me and rest your legs," Ohayaa said. "The afterbirth can just plop into the hole."

Though as agonizing as her last contractions, gazing at her new baby distracted her from the effort. Once she delivered the placenta, Tʉe Tseenaʔ mashed on her belly to ensure every piece had come loose, and then wrapped it in buckskin. Eva grimaced under her sister's wrenching hand.

With that critical task complete, Ohayaa washed her legs before they moved her to the bed, and Eva sighed in contentment to be able to rest on her back.

When the cord stopped pulsing, Tʉe Tseenaʔ cut it, leaving several inches between the end and the baby's stomach, and wrapped it tightly against her new son with buckskin. "Let's get some broth into you," she said when she was done.

Ohayaa asked if she could bathe the baby, and Eva handed him up reluctantly. "So many boys," Ohayaa said once he was in her arms. "We need a girl next to even things out!"

"Not from me," Eva said. "I'm never doing that again."

Tʉe Tseenaʔ and Ohayaa just laughed. "Your body will forget," Tʉe Tseenaʔ said. "We're made to forget the suffering; otherwise, there'd be no humans. Even now, when I watched, my mind remembers I felt pain birthing Tʉe Kahuu, and I can recite the feeling words, but my body holds no memory. I remember exactly what it felt like to break my little finger once, but the birth… it's like a dark hole. It's very strange. A blessing, though, I think. We women endure something men will never have to face."

"Can you imagine Rʉtsima?" Ohayaa asked with a laugh.

"Or Pasahòo," Tʉe Tseenaʔ said.

Eva understood now why her ancestors believed women who died in childbirth went to Valhalla. She had never felt more like a warrior. As her body adjusted, she shivered uncontrollably, and Tʉe Tseenaʔ covered her with several warm blankets.

"You did well, Nami," she said, placing her forehead against Eva's and smiling. "We didn't even need the medicine woman."

"May I have some meat?"

"Sorry, no meat until your confinement is over," Tʉe Tseenaʔ said. "It'll make you bleed too much. But we'll feed you other good things that will make lots of milk."

Ravenous, Eva's stomach growled.

"Do I hear a baby crying?" Rʉtsima called through the brush wall. A grandfather always asked the sex of the child as soon as possible, but Jim's elder brother seemed happy to fill that role since their father's death. His excited voice danced with impatience. "Wives! What is it?"

"It is your close friend," Ohayaa said.

Knowing she meant a boy, Rʉtsima whooped loud enough to wake the entire village.

Jim loped next to Kuhtu in the light of a full summer moon. For the first time in his life, he didn't want to be on a raid. He jerked his war pony's reins and came to a complete stop.

Kuhtu halted a dozen yards ahead and trotted back. The rest of their raiding party continued on, unaware.

"I'm going back."

"Why? You can't see Eva or the baby for ten days. Raiding will take your mind off her."

"I don't want to take my mind off her. I want to be near, even if I can't see her. I can at least hear the baby cry when it's born."

"You really want to turn back from a war party without engaging the enemy?"

"I don't care," Jim said. "People know my war record." He turned his stallion's head without waiting for his true friend's agreement, but the hoof-beats of Kuhtu's horse fell into sync with his own.

As they reentered the sleeping village and walked toward the birthing lodge, they heard a long whoop, and Jim took off at a run. As soon as his brother was within view, he shouted, "What is it?"

"A boy!" Rʉtsima stood a safe distance away from the power-soaked lodge and turned his face back to the wall. "Healthy? Baby and Eva?"

"Yes," Tʉe Tseenaʔ replied. "Go away and let us be. We have much to do."

Rʉtsima shook his head at his second wife's tone but smiled nonetheless as he stepped toward Jim and his friend. "She will be a powerful medicine woman. She's a different person when she is midwifing."

Jim rounded the lodge to the western wall and dropped his voice. "Eva?"

"Jim?"

"Are you well?"

"I didn't tear." She sounded relieved and excited, but he widened his eyes in horror at her words. He had no idea what happened in a birthing hut.

More words tumbled from her mouth, gaining speed. "We have a son! He's beautiful. And perfect. I wish you could hold him. I wish you could have been with me. Why aren't you raiding?"

"I needed to be near you," he said in English. "I've never wished more to be Anglo again. I would be at your side now." The urge to break down the branches to meet his child and kiss his wife rose in his arms, and he forced his hands behind his back.

"It's not safe," Eva said, surprising him.

"Your puha has never overpowered mine." The baby gave a soft cry, and he heard Eva rustling on the other side of the brush.

"I think, this time, it might, Husband," she replied in Comanche with overawed fear in her voice. "I respect what Tʉe Tseenaʔ says we need to do."

"Your wife was very brave, Husband, and your son is strong and healthy," Tʉe Tseenaʔ said. "You should be very proud. Go rejoin your war party. We will take good care of your wife, and when you return, she will be able to greet you."

Jim smirked at her directive. "I will be back on day ten. No later."

When he returned to his friends, he clapped Rʉtsima on the shoulder. "Choose a powerful name for my new son, Elder Brother. When the time is right, I would have you give him his formal one."

"I would be honored, Younger Brother," he said, returning his embrace. "Now, go. Bring back many horses to give away in celebration of his and Eva's health. I will watch over our women." He turned his face to Kuhtu. "Keep him busy."

"I've been trying. Come on, Haitsi̱. We still have time to catch up with them on the trail."

Ten days had never passed more slowly for any man; Jim was sure of it. Even as he led horses out of barns on silent feet, he thought of Eva and wondered what she and the baby were doing right at that very moment. On day seven, he said, “We should head back.”

“It’s only a day and a half ride home. Tops,” Kuhtu said. “Even at a comfortable speed. No, we are not going back yet.”

On day eight, Jim said, “I’m going.”

Kuhtu sighed. “It’s probably for the best. You’re so distracted; we’re lucky you haven’t gotten us killed.”

They bid farewell to their war leader, and Jim pushed them as if they had enemies at their heels.

On day nine, Kuhtu forced them to stop outside the village and camp overnight. “You can’t see her yet. Or the baby.”

After he hobbled his horses, Jim glowered and paced around the campfire.

“Just kill me if I ever feel this way about a woman,” Kuhtu said, dragging a blanket over his ears to drown out Jim’s annoying behavior.

Jim kicked a stone at his back. “Just wait until it’s your first child. Then we’ll see how you act.”

From under the covering, Kuhtu’s muffled voice said, “Tʉe Tseenaʔ would skin me alive if I bring you back too soon.”

Finally, the sun rose on day ten, and Jim had his horse saddled, as well as Kuhtu's, before his friend even awoke.

"Let's go. No more delays. It's day ten."

"At least bathe, Haitsi̱," Kuhtu said. "Your woman isn't going to want a smelly Anglo hugging her."

Only Kuhtu could get away with saying something like that to him, but he had a point.

As soon as they were ready, they led their stolen prizes behind them and entered the village. The first man they came across asked after the health of Pasahòo's new baby, and Jim told him to take his pick of the horses he had brought.

Kuhtu continued to his own kahni, and Jim galloped to Eva's birthing hut but found it empty, which was a good sign. At a trot, he headed to the river, stopping and scanning the banks. Not seeing her right away, Jim followed downstream. Eventually, he stumbled onto Tʉe Tseenaʔ, who sat near a cradleboard while Eva soaked in a swirling eddy.

"Husband!" Tʉe Tseenaʔ said, looking up.

Eva's eyes opened, and an enormous smile lit her face.

"Come meet your son," Tʉe Tseenaʔ said, drawing his eyes back to the cradleboard.

Overwhelmed with sudden shyness, Jim dismounted and asked, "Can I take him out?"

Tʉe Tseenaʔ chuckled. "Of course. He's your son." She showed him how to unlace the tight bindings, and once free, the baby scrunched his tiny red face and fists in sleep and arched his back in a stretch.

Nerves made Jim's hands stiff, and he held his breath as Tʉe Tseenaʔ laid his new child in the cradle of his arms. When he gazed down, a wave of contentment spread a peaceful balm on his soul, and he nearly cried. After a moment, he curled his strong body over his baby's fragile one and touched his lips to his downy brow, memorizing his smell.

He beamed at his brother's wife. "This is my son."

"Yes," she said, grinning back. She gave Jim a warm, parting hug, and he expressed his gratitude as she walked up and over the bank.

He found Eva's eyes and stepped to the edge of the water. "I missed you."

"I missed you, too."

"Are you able to join me on the blanket?"

A strange look came over her face, and she turned the color of a cardinal. "I don't look the way I used to. The way I did before I was pregnant."

"What do you mean?"

Avoiding his gaze, she stood up.

Before him, he saw his wife's gorgeous body. Though looser, it looked much the same as before she entered confinement. Puzzled, he asked, "What's wrong?"

"I thought my belly would go down."

"It will. Ohayaa's and Tʉe Tseenaʔ's did. Until then, I love that part of you, too. It gave us our son."

Eva met his eyes and waded to him.

He held out his hand, and she let him help her up the bank. "Come here, Wife." Jim tugged her wet body to him for a deep kiss, their child between them.

After a moment, he released her to dress in her best clothes.

"I think you were supposed to let me return to you at our kahni," she said.

"I couldn't wait." While she told him about the birth, he settled on the blanket to watch and marveled at the day.

"Tʉe Tseenaʔ gave me heat treatments to slow my bleeding. She warmed the earth with coals, then raked them away so I could lie down on my belly. It felt so good. Except for the fact you couldn't be in there with me, I would never have come out of the birthing lodge. Oh, and look," she said, opening the baby's wrappings. "His cord fell off yesterday. Tʉe Tseenaʔ hid it in a hackberry tree. He'll have a long life if no one finds it."

Right here, on the banks of the Colorado, Jim had everything he could have ever wanted. He had regained what he had lost in Goliad, including his strength, and Eva's heart had healed. She sat next to him, and he gazed in wonder at her face, the clear sky behind her head shifting her gray-green eyes to a brilliant blue.

"Are you happy?" she asked.

"Yes. Are you?"

"Yes." She caressed their baby's cheek with a rounded finger. "I didn't know such love could exist before I met you… and now him."

Jim placed his forehead against her own and breathed in her clean scent. "Fate brought you to me."

"Maybe so, but I chose to stay."

The adventure continues in *The Time Mender Dispatch: News from the Temporal Front*. For new releases and other time travel happenings, get your copy of Lux Libera's regular periodical by signing up here:

https://jennifermarchman.com/list

If you enjoyed reading *The Guardian*, I always appreciate reviews! They mean everything to independent authors like me. The Amazon search algorithm favors books with many reviews, which means more readers can find my work, and I can keep writing. Please consider leaving one on Amazon, Goodreads, or BookBub.

And I love, love, love hearing from readers! For links to contact me, view fun extras, sign up for my newsletter, or leave a review for *The Guardian*, please visit:

https://jennifermarchman.com/tgc

Reading a print copy? Use your phone's camera to follow the link:

Notes & Acknowledgments

Addendum to Book 1 & 2's Author's Notes & Acknowledgments

Full notes available at:
https://jennifermarchman.com/authors-note

Anglo Society

San Felipe's residents start panicking ahead of the Runaway Scrape a little earlier in Jim's timeline than they did in ours. Rumors began trickling in that the Alamo had fallen over March 15th and 16th, but the fact wasn't confirmed until the 17th with the arrival of Houston's aide-de-camp bringing the news, though the Runaway Scrape had already begun in towns south of San Felipe. Those who waited too long to evacuate lost their wagons to Houston. I want to thank Bryan McAuley, Site Manager at the San Felipe de Austin State Historic Site, for corresponding with me.

T'ibek'a

The guardian sect of T'ibek'a is based on the real guardian of the Ark of the Covenant in Aksum, Ethiopia, and the churches of Lalibela, a world wonder. I want to thank my dear friend, Ezana Haile, for helping me with the Amharic translations.

When Kidisti places the food in Eva's mouth, she is offering garusha, an act of love, honor, and respect with many social layers and nuanced meanings. To offer garusha to an enemy shows great compassion and opens a door for forgiveness and redemption.

Battle of Coleto Creek & the Goliad Massacre

The seed of this book came from learning about the Angel of Goliad while my seventh grader studied Texas history, and we visited the museum at Presidio-La Bahía in Goliad, TX. Her story deserves to be better known.

There is extraordinarily little information about the Goliad Massacre, and I relied heavily on Jay A. Stout's book *Slaughter at Goliad: The Mexican Massacre of 400 Texas Volunteers*. I'd also like to thank him for my favorite email exchange while researching this book.

The Sons of DeWitt Colony website proved to be a fantastic treasure trove of primary sources and is considered by the museum at Presidio-La Bahía to be a credible source of information.

I'd also like to thank Scott McMahon, Director Presidio-La Bahía, for corresponding with me on several questions. And while I speak some Spanish, I need to thank my friend Felicitas Cadena for answering my random translation questions as they came up.

Though Will and Daniel are fictional characters, everyone else at Goliad was a real person. Ehrenberg survived the firing squad and wrote some of our best accounts of that day. Bill Hunter, a man mentioned briefly when Jim first arrives at the fort, feigned death, but was discovered, bayoneted, and left for dead during the looting. After night fell, he crawled to the San Antonio River to hide. If you want to know the rest of his story, you'll have to read Jay's book. Unfortunately, most of the Greys, including Noah, were killed, though Spanish-speaking Spohn was spared execution at the last minute because someone noticed he had gotten in line to march.

Francisca went on to save more Texians and provided materially for their aid and comfort. When she returned to Mexico City, Telesforo abandoned her penniless. No one really knows her actual name, but she should be remembered for her extraordinary compassion and relentless courage.

Sources:

Books:

- Gary Brown. *Volunteers in the Texas Revolution: The New Orleans Greys*. Plano: Wordware Publishing, 1999.

- Ornish, Natalie. *Ehrenberg: Goliad Survivor,*

Old West Explorer: a Biography, With the First Complete Scholarly Translation of The Fight for Freedom in Texas in the Year 1836. Dallas: Texas Heritage Press, 1997.

- Stout, Jay A. *Slaughter at Goliad: The Mexican Massacre of 400 Texas Volunteers.* Annapolis: Naval Institute Press, 2008.

Websites:

- "Map of Fannin's Fight, March 19, 1836." Map of Fannin's Fight, March 19, 1836 | Texas State Library and Archives Commission. Accessed July 15, 2021. https://www.tsl.texas.gov/treasures/republic/goliad/fannin-map1.html

- Sons of DeWitt Colony, Texas. Accessed July 15, 2021. http://www.sonsofdewittcolony.org/

Support the Goliad State Park & Historic Site

Goliad State Park and Historic Site are preserving the history of the Texas Revolution and the memory of the men who died there. Please consider supporting their mission.

- https://tpwd.texas.gov/state-parks/goliad/goliad-area-historic-sites

Translations

Spanish

Soldados — Soldiers
Uno momento, por favor. — One moment, please.
Todos ustedes van. — You all go.
Vamanos. — Let's go.
Por favor — Please
Gracias — Thank you
Ándale — Quickly
Cállate — Shut up
Jacales — Huts
¿Quien habla español? — Who speaks Spanish?
Perdón, señor. Repita, por favor. — Pardon, sir. Repeat, please.
Agua — Water
Canalla — Scoundrel
Bandas blancas — White bands
Arrodillarse. — Kneel down.
¿Quien habla español? — Who speaks Spanish?

French

Et voilà. — And there you go.
Ma crotte — My dropping
Monsieur — Sir
S'il vous plaît — Please

Nʉmʉ tekwapʉ̲ (Comanche)

For a pronunciation guide, visit
https://jennifermarchman.com/translations
(or the Comanche Language Department's website:
https://www.talkcomanche.org/
At the time of this writing, there is no pronunciation guide on their website, but I hope that changes in the future.)

Haʔii! — Oh my!
Nami — Younger Sister

German

Kommen bitte übersetzen. — Come please translate.
Fräulein — Miss, a young, unmarried woman

Amharic

Menik'esak'esi āyasifeligimi. — No need to move.
T'ibek'a — Protection, the act of doing the protection
Tebaki — Guard (singular)Tebakiyochi — Guards

Also by Jennifer Marchman

The Mender Trilogy

The Mender – Book 1
The Captive – Book 2
The Guardian – Book 3

Short Stories

"The Hunt"

The Accidental Time Travelers Collective, Volume One
- an anthology by 12 time-traveling authors
"Field and Flame" (a prequel to the Mender Trilogy)

For an up-to-date list of Jennifer's publications visit:
https://jennifermarchman.com/alsoby

For new releases and other time travel happenings, join Jennifer's mailing list, the *Time Mender Dispatch: News from the Temporal Front,* at jennifermarchman.com/list

About the Author

Jennifer Marchman lives in Austin, Texas, with her husband, three nearly grown children, and the two best dogs in the world. At different times, she has worn various authorial hats, including ghostwriter-memoirist, editor, curriculum writer, educational blogger, grant writer, and addicted social media over-sharer, but now, after many years, she's writing for pleasure.

Jennifer is a member of the Writers' League of Texas, the Historical Novel Society, and #TimeTravelAuthors in the Twitterverse. She enjoys flamenco dancing, is the proud owner of a white belt in jiu-jitsu, and wishes to compete internationally in mounted archery but lacks a ticket to Kazakhstan and a horse to practice on. She has toyed with the idea of picking up pottery again, but needs more hours in her day and a husband willing to install (for the fourth time) the necessary electrical outlet for a kiln that may likely go unused.

Though she is not sure, she probably would have run off at the age of twelve to be a time traveler — if the opportunity had presented itself.

Jennifer's debut novel, *The Mender*, is a 2022 finalist in the Writers' League of Texas Manuscript Contest.

Want to read more from the multiverse of *The Mender,* find pre-order links for new books, learn about Jennifer, join her reader group, or follow her on social media?

Visit her website at:
jennifermarchman.com

Made in United States
Cleveland, OH
15 April 2025

16133205R00171